HER PRIVATE JOHN

Betty Womack

EROTIC ROMANCE

Siren Publishing, Inc.
www.SirenPublishing.com

A SIREN PUBLISHING BOOK
IMPRINT: Erotic Romance

HER PRIVATE JOHN

ISBN-10: 1-60601-509-5
ISBN-13: 978-1-60601-509-4

First Printing: June 2009

Cover design by Jinger Heaston

Printed in the U.S.A.

PUBLISHER
Siren Publishing, Inc.
www.SirenPublishing.com

HER PRIVATE JOHN

BETTY WOMACK

Chapter One

Bella Cantatore caught the scent of John's cologne wafting to her like a seductive whisper as she walked by his side. She hated John Breten Lawless. Hated the clothes he wore, right down to the Italian suit that draped his broad shoulders and hinted at the promise of strength in his long, muscular legs.

God, he was a big man.

Her lips softened into a playful smile as she checked out the razor sharp creases in his trousers, and their perfect length, the hem falling in one fold across the instep of his spit-polished British Walkers. Against her last bit of will, her gaze moved to the area of his tight rear. Sure, it was hidden under his suit coat now, but how many times had she eyeballed his nice derriere while he leaned over her chair to hand something to her grandfather, or stood with his hands in his pockets?

Well, she didn't exactly hate him. Her feelings for him were so deep and strong it was sinful. Their lives had touched for the first time four years earlier. And her heart and soul had committed to the foolish desire to have him for her own. Crazy girl.

She remembered the way his deep turquoise gaze had taken in every detail of her body before lifting to her face that day. He had experienced the same jolt of discovery that she had, but that all vanished when her grandfather blurted out they were celebrating her birthday. Her seventeenth birthday. John looked as if he had been goosed in the crotch with a cattle prod.

Thinking about the grief they had caused one another made her pulse race. She desperately needed a drink of water. She let him get a step ahead of her as they walked in icy silence down the long hallway to her attorney's office.

John turned back to gaze down at her with a silent snarl in his eyes. Her lips twitched with a poorly hidden grin, caused by the self-deprecating idea that being this close to her made him nervous. He had a razor nick on his chin. He stared at her for a moment longer before speaking.

"I hope you lose that surly attitude before we see Max." He eyed her as if she were a misbehaving kid.

The secretive smile on her lips was that of a woman having pleasure at a man's expense. He probably knew she had been giving him the hot once-over, but didn't flinch a well-toned muscle under her perusal. Still the tough Navy pilot, sworn to treat her like a non-com. But, oh yes. He'd felt it, felt the stroke of her desire touching his hard body.

"Why, John. I haven't been surly for several years." She skillfully tucked her elbow to her side when he tried to cup his hand around it. "They call it adult independence these days. I'll see myself in."

"Sorry to mess up your show of independence, Flower, but for some strange reason, I was asked to be here for the reading of the will." His gaze was speculative. "You wouldn't know anything about this, would you?"

His use of her middle name in what she considered a vulgar fashion irked her. "It's Fleur. Of course, a man with few social skills wouldn't know that. And you're probably lying about being asked to be here."

Anger flared in the depths of his green eyes and his white teeth showed in a hard grimace. "Listen, you spoiled hardhead. I don't give a damn about you or what you do after today." He flicked at the fragile netting on her navy snap-brim hat and smiled sardonically. "This is the last tour of duty I pull with you, Flower."

He had called her Flower, his way of telling her he was ticked off. He must be boiling now. She did what he hated most. She laughed at his anger, fueling his temper. "I know you want me. And you know it will never happen."

His chiseled lips set in a hard line and his eyes took on the color of a storm tossed sea—deep, dark and dangerously green. He caught her arm and leaned against her, whispering in her ear.

"Only in your most erotic dream, Flower."

Electricity crackled between them, arcing from his hand to her trembling body. He had unwittingly hit upon a taboo subject, the thing she hated most about him. Those incessant erotic dreams she'd been having since her eighteenth birthday, and where he was the recipient of her favors. Three years of rolling around in bed, only to wake up clinging to her pillow, expecting to find him beside her.

Why was she still warring with this man? She was twenty-one, had a wonderful job as an antiquities expert and had a great place to live. Plus, she was not without male company. Damn him for making her do inventory on her crazy life as if she had to please him. She snatched her wayward emotions back in time to avoid another sparring match with John.

With his hand gripping her elbow, she walked inside the office that had been a playground for her as a child. Maxwell Fortis had been her grandfather's closest friend and attorney. Between her grandfather and Maxwell, she had gotten everything she wanted. Except one thing.

She started towards Max's private office, but John held her back and gave their names to the receptionist.

"Bella Cantatore and John Lawless to see Mr. Fortis."

Wearying of his parental like control, Bella shrugged away from him. "You can leave now. Go back to your little brokerage office, flirt with your saucy secretary."

"You're enough sauce for anyone to stand in a lifetime."

He dropped Bella's arm and they chose to sit at opposite ends of the tastefully furnished room, rich with walnut bookcases and gleaming oak floors. The room catered to both male and female with a variety of soft leather armchairs and cut velvet couches.

Bella thumbed through a magazine and observed him from beneath her lashes, wanting to throw the magazine at his dark head. She huffed softly. He did look good, no use denying that. Eyeing his deep tan, a sliver of jealousy pierced her heart. It was obvious he'd spent a lot of time at the pool this summer.

She imagined he spent even more time picking up women. The bastard would chase anything in a skirt. She grimaced, realizing her thoughts were based purely on envy. Bella had seen him with several different women, but to her disappointment, none of them looked like tramps. She was curious about the women he dated. Mad dog jealous was more like it

Disgust streaked through her when she thought about the amount of time and care she had put into getting perfumed, oiled and polished for this face to face with the man she hated. Six months had passed since her grandfather died and their meetings had been accidental and pointedly brief.

It struck her like a cold wind, the fact she might never see John after today. There would be no reason for them to be in the same place. He had his 'elderly' friends, as she called them, and her crowd was all too carefree to hang with old John. Her soft snort of derision made John look up from his magazine. *Oh, yeah. You would notice that.*

"Bella?"

"John?"

"You were staring at me. Do you want to say something?"

"I couldn't possibly say it in mixed company." Damn. He was so good at catching her whenever she slipped into that fog-like trance of staring at him. She averted her gaze from temptation and his sexy smile.

She knew her state of denial was bordering on psychotic. The past six months of near separation had done nothing to alter the fact he was the one. She'd known it the first moment his green eyes had met and held her bold stare. Well, it had become a deep, unshakable and completely unrequited devotion on her part. Over the past four years, it had become a quest to hurt him. It hadn't worked. He seemed to find her more resistible at every turn.

He exhaled as if he were bored. *Well, hell, you don't have to be bored, Johnny. It's more fun over here.* Her breath caught in her throat. Their glances clashed in a duel of wills. She refused to give ground this time. The battle ended when the receptionist intervened.

"Mr. Fortis will see you both now." She started to lead the way.

John stood and waited for Bella to get to her feet, pasting on his best smile as he spoke to the receptionist. "We'll find it. Thank you."

Bella gave him a hard glare and brushed at her skirt. "Does he have to go in with me? I'd prefer he didn't."

The primly dressed receptionist darted a beleaguered glance from Bella to John. "I'm sorry. I'll see if Mr. Fortis will see you separately."

"She's joking." John gripped Bella's wrist and squeezed. "We'll just go in now."

He steered Bella in the direction the nervous receptionist had gestured. Before he could get her through the door to Max's private office, she pulled back.

"Do you mind? You've had your hands all over me."

"Bella," he murmured, "we can trade insults later. Now isn't the right time for it."

"We'll do nothing later."

"Promise?"

After he ushered her into the office, he shook hands with Max. The two men immediately fell into a conversation about the price of sweet crude, seeming to forget she was alive. Damn.

It was common knowledge John didn't like her, but he was being downright rude. The next second, he reached back and pulled her forward to stand beside him.

"Sorry, Bella."

Even that belated apology was far out of the norm for him. She leaned over to accept a kiss on the cheek from Max.

He patted her shoulder and hugged her. "You look lovely as always, honey. Have a seat and I'll get you a coffee."

John spoke up, apparently trying to hurry things along. "So, Max." He took a cigar that the attorney offered. "Bella and I are both in kind of a rush to get back to our lives. Can we get started?"

Bella laid her handbag on the desk and took a seat. John sat beside her, lit his cigar and looked bored. Catching her frown of annoyance, he took a deep drag on his cigar and blew a huge smoke ring over her head.

"Want one, Flower?"

She rolled her eyes and pointed to her handbag. "Thanks, but I have my own." She didn't mind the aroma of cigars. Max hadn't caved to public opinion. The office was still a smoker's place. He and John belonged to the same club where they went to enjoy their exorbitantly expensive tobacco and cognac.

Max placed a cup of coffee in front of Bella and straightened the stacks of papers on his desk before sitting down to read the will of her grandfather, Roman Marcus Cantatore.

The folder was thick with pages of legal documents, and her mind wandered during the lengthy process. It was all mumbo jumbo to her. Max's voice had become a drone and she paid scant attention to what was being said, until she heard the words that made her sit forward in her chair.

"What?" She blinked several times. "I'm sorry. I think I misunderstood the last part of what you said." Glancing at John confirmed her suspicion as to what she had heard. He was staring a fiery hole through her and clenching that cigar between his teeth. "I have to marry to inherit, and it has to be to John Lawless?"

Max looked at her over the hefty folder. "That's what Roman wanted, Bella."

Her laughter flowed soft as snowfall, yet she had wanted it to sound harsh. This was a typical joke pulled by her grandfather. "Roman must have been liquored to the gills or insane when he drew this up."

"Oh, no. I assure you he was in perfect control of his faculties. I'll just go over the fine print for you again." Max cleared his throat and began reading aloud again. "Bella. 'Bella Fleur Cantatore, my granddaughter, will inherit forty-two and a half million dollars, the family home in Farmer's Branch, and the old homestead ranch outside Dallas, provided Bella marries John Breten Lawless.'"

A deep silence permeated the room until Max continued reading.

"'This marriage will be treated as a loving union for a period of six months. The couple will live together in the same home. If, after this period, they do not wish to remain together, the marriage can be dissolved or annulled. If all these conditions are met to the best of their ability, Bella Fleur Cantatore will become the sole heir of the estate of Roman Marcus Cantatore.'"

Bella wondered if her face was scarlet, mortified by the contents of the will. "This is one of my grandfather's tricks, isn't it?"

Max held his hand up to gain her attention. "There's an additional requirement. I quote his words here, 'Bella will sit on the board of directors of the Cantatore Brokerage Firm during this time, acting as the tie-breaking vote on the board. She will relinquish that seat at the end of six months.'"

Out of patience and trying to control her temper, Bella stood up and stared at Max as if he had grown two heads and a tail. "That's absurd. I'm an antiquities archeologist." Grabbing her handbag, she gave her final thoughts on the subject. "The whole thing is disgusting. I won't be paired with a pasture bull like some prize heifer."

Max eyed her over the papers in his hand. "There‘s more, and I quote, ‘In the event Bella does not abide by the terms, she will be allotted a stipend of five thousand dollars a year.’" He looked past Bella to the silent party sitting in the chair beside her. "John, I’m sure you’ll want to hear the final paragraph of the will. It states, ‘In the event Bella Fleur Cantatore does not agree to become the lawful wife of John Breten Lawless, the estate of Roman Marcus Cantatore will become the uncontested property of the State of Texas to use at the discretion of the duly elected judges.’"

Until that moment, John had sat in dispassionate silence, smoking his cigar. Now, he was on his feet and casually slid one hand into his pocket, leaning around Bella to flick ash from his cigar.

"What the hell was that, Max?" He ground the cigar out and curled his fingers around her arm, turning his full glare on Bella. "This is the most harebrained scheme you've ever hatched, and I'll damn well not be sucker punched by you or your grandpa."

Her mouth opened and a soft laugh flowed out. "It figures you would assume I dictated this revolting, moronic bit of crap to my grandfather."

John's smile was more of a grimace. "You forget, I know you better than anyone." He turned to Max. "Can we be alone for a few minutes?"

Max stood and headed for the door. "Of course. I’ll go wash my hands." He left and gave them the privacy of the office.

Her fingers busied themselves in the strands of hair that were tickling her neck. "So, what did you mean by that last comment, exactly?"

"Nervous, are we?" he murmured in her ear and grinned at her. His arm brushed hers and he fixed his gaze with hers. "It means, when you want something, you’ll stop at nothing to get it."

She tried to convey supreme modulated disgust. "You’re too vain. Do you really think I couldn't have put the ring in your nose any time I wanted and with no resistance at all?"

Leaning a fraction closer, he chuckled. "I've never met a woman with such arrogance and nothing to back it up." His gaze fastened on her mouth. "Honey, you're the last one I'd let throw a saddle on my back."

"Don't fret. I prefer a man when I want company." She couldn't help the way her tongue flicked out to wet her lips.

"Okay. Cool off." John walked over to the window and stared out of it for a brief time before coming back to Bella. "Come outside and I'll buy you a drink."

Her hackles rose at his invitation, like she was some vanquished competition. "I wasn't good enough for you three years ago. What's changed?"

"Jesus Christ." He laughed down at her. "I didn't ask for anything but a drink."

Desire to irritate him would not allow her to be silent. "Go on and leave. I'm positive I saw one of your dates being released from the police station on the way down here."

He rubbed the back of his neck and scowled at her. "Bella, you're talking like a back alley cat."

She faltered. She didn't like being a bitch. Her coarse personality was reserved for him alone and she hated it. Yet, she couldn't let him insult her without retaliating.

"That's the only language you understand."

As usual, the rest of the world had to wait while Bella and John spoke their minds.

His jaw clenched as he leaned closer to her and the color of his eyes deepened. "You've had that bullshit attitude of yours ever since you were a horny teenager."

Her lashes fluttered down to conceal the screaming emotional turmoil in her heart. "No, it all started when you decided to wreck my life."

He gave her a wry smile and caught her fingers in his hand. "You were screwing a man old enough to be your father."

"He was twenty-one, and we were not screwing." Her shoulder pressed to his arm.

"You would've." He dropped her hand and averted his gaze somewhere over her head.

Bella's heart ached to let her rampaging hurts and fears loose on him, but she drew on her force field of cool reserve. He didn't get it then and he didn't get it now.

Remembering what had happened at that moment in their lives, she wondered how dumb one man could be. Who had made the call to tell him where she was on that eventful night? She had. And what did he say to her? Nothing. Just threw his coat around her to conceal her identity and hustled her out the back door of the Dallas hotel. She sighed and looked away from his stony profile.

"Did it matter to you, John?" The question had been asked calmly, but she was dying to know his feelings. That night at the hotel, she had wanted him to berate her, to tell her he was worried or jealous. But he hadn't. He didn't care about her at all.

"Damn straight. Roman made me your shadow as part of my duties while I worked for him. And I was well-paid to harass you."

Her voice lowered as she slowly unbuttoned the top button of her suit jacket. "You did a thorough job. Ruined my first year of college and kept me virginal for a while."

He studied her through narrowed eyes and grinned. "There is some doubt about that one."

"Virginity is overrated." She loved the scent of his cologne, rich and heady with sea heather and exotic spices.

His voice had a husky timbre when he spoke. "It looked good on you."

As quickly as it began, it was over. John touched her shoulder and took several steps toward the door. Max came back into the room and stopped his leaving.

"Now look here, children. You didn't let me finish. This is an important matter." He adjusted his glasses and read the final bit of the will. "'Bella must meet the immediate terms within ten days of this date or action will be taken to make the state the beneficiary.'"

Bella turned her back on the two men and shivered. What had possessed her grandfather to go this far? Sure, there had been a few off hand comments passed between her and Roman about how much he admired John and how good a husband he would be for some lucky girl. But she had never said it was what she wanted.

This was way over what she and Roman had talked about. He had full knowledge that John couldn't stand her and that she despised John. More than the inheritance, the idea of coercing John into marrying her was the lowest kind of bribery. Lord. She couldn't bring herself to be bought and sold for any amount of money.

John glanced at Max before he grabbed her wrist and pulled Bella to a small alcove for a final modicum of privacy. "Get off your high horse or you'll be checking out grub at the nearest food mart. And, get this through your head. I am not going to marry you to pull your sweet ass out of the fire." He eased his grip and murmured against her ear. "Try to work something out with Max."

"Bella?" Max called to her.

She shook her head. Her voice was strong. "Don't ask me to crawl to John for anything. I'm not doing it."

"This is too important to be stubborn." Max sounded agitated. "You have to settle it and soon."

John looked intently at her, saying nothing for a time and then lifted an eyebrow as if he got her message. "I believe she's made her decision, Max."

She heard his deep intake of breath and his footsteps as he walked out of the room. He left Bella where she stood, left her in real doubt about her handling of the scheme she realized now had been thought up by her grandfather, Roman. John would never go for such a horrible trick. Because of her meddling grandfather, she would probably never see John again.

Why couldn't John just love her? She had never thought to use trickery but the idea didn't seem to be so bad right now. No, John found her to be too much of a challenge. From the first day they clapped eyes on one another four years ago, he had maintained his hands off policy. Obviously, he still felt the same today.

She lifted her head, squared her shoulders and took a gold cased lipstick from her purse to freshen her makeup. Never look desperate or needy. She clamped her lips tight to subdue the little sound of agony in her throat while her teary gaze followed John's departure. If he came back, it would have to be his decision.

Chapter Two

When had he begun to see Bella as a desirable bed partner? The subject galled and perplexed John. He detested admitting even to himself that it had been from the first moment their eyes met four years ago.

Since that first encounter, he had undergone a tremendous storm of sexual tension that should have killed him. And she had enjoyed every second of his misery. If he had been smart and not such a gentleman, she would have gotten what they both wanted and screwed the attraction out of their blood.

But he hadn't been willing to sleep with a girl that needed a lullaby more than down and dirty sex. He preferred women with some miles on their odometer and didn't need directions on where to put it. Added to the mix was his real friendship with Roman, making a hot sex-only affair with Bella out of the question. He still had some honor left. Then there was the thing of being Roman's friend.

The thought of being in confinement with Bella for six months frankly scared him. He'd made it a full time job to steel his body against wanting her and he wasn't even sure he could satisfy her. Not that he'd ever had complaints. And, not that she wanted him for sex. No, he was sure she had plenty of sex with experienced foreigners that knew how to please a chick with a frigging feather or a camelhair brush implanted in their prick. Hell, he wasn't ever going that far. If his stuff wasn't enough, she could go somewhere else.

John took a swig of his beer and grimaced. Sure, he'd wanted to screw her, but he'd wanted a lot of women and survived without accomplishing his goal.

The immediate dilemma had only one solution. Harsh reality hit. The allotted time to do something about the problem he was certain Bella had created was running out. Eight days had slipped by without hearing a peep from her.

He should have seen it coming. Roman wanted him in the Cantatore family business and had made sure that it happened. The sharp-minded old fox had no compunction about using bribery or trickery to further his own interests. Hell of it was, Bella had probably made some smart-ass remark about wanting John and Roman had sunk his teeth in like a Gila monster. No, he couldn't go soft on her now. It hadn't been that way at all. She had probably just asked Roman to buy him.

The beer bottle in his hand was getting warm. He set it on the bar and walked to the sliding glass doors that opened onto his terrace. He groaned and pulled the cord to close the drapes against the setting sun that poured in through the glass doors.

Before they were completely drawn, his gaze drifted down to the apartment complex pool. A nubile lovely in a dental floss sized suit lay stretched out on a yellow plastic raft, her legs spread in utter relaxation.

His interest was minimal. Damn it. Bella had dehorned him. It seemed his whoring days were well behind him. He hadn't had sex in months. For some reason, his balls wouldn't warm up to anyone but Flower. Their dedication to her had been established the last time he had picked her up at the airport after one of her job related trips. She'd been away for two months, somewhere in Spain. That night, he'd stupidly tried to flirt with her. She ignored his overture of romance and carried on a mushy, long distance phone conversation with some bastard she'd known in Spain.

How frigging dumb of him to let his guard down. Bella was a hot babe and she couldn't see him for dust. Oh, she liked playing with his libido, making him hard, but she didn't see him as anything but a thorn in her butt. He yanked the drapes together.

Noticing the bottle of Chardonnay on the coffee table, he cursed out loud. "Damn it. Whoring? Not you, buddy." He was supposed to have dinner with a woman he barely knew. The wine was for her and the hope she would be in the mood for fast, hard and frequent sex. Which would it be? The planned-for certain sex or Bella and her knee to his balls?

Leaning against the bar in his living room, he hashed over his choices. *Okay, Lawless. What are you going to do about Bella? You would love to teach her a lesson in humility, but she doesn't deserve to be left wondering if she'll have more than pocket change next week.* He sure as hell didn't need or want her money.

He picked up the phone. Roman would have loved all the sweat and hot tempers and sleepless nights his asinine will had caused. Now there were two days left and the thing had taken on new and serious consequences. John had made up his mind. And he had to do the right thing by Bella. And, he might have some fun putting her through humility training. Damn it.

After a hasty call of sorry excuses to his dinner date, he changed from a suit into worn Levi’s and a white T-shirt. He worked up a sweat while tying his shoes. It must have been a fever making him nuts enough to go ask the gorgeous wench from hell to marry him.

This particular trial in his life had begun soon after he’d crashed his motorcycle on loose gravel outside the Pensacola Naval Air Station. The lousy concussion he got out of the deal had put him on the vertigo washout list. He'd become a loser at twenty-five. No more flying the big bomber he loved. One hard earned commission and a career down the drain.

Yeah, he had been bitter and at loose ends. The ugly feeling of uncertainty still caught him off guard at times. And like some psycho, to keep his ugly, painful memories vivid, he'd brought that damned motorcycle to Texas.

His biggest mistake had been in not going back to the welcoming arms of his family in Austin. They had just the position waiting for him in his father's brokerage firm, and the right girl, according to his mother.

None of this would be happening if he'd swallowed his pride and gone on home. Heaving another rough groan of dread, he picked up his keys and wallet and left the safety of his apartment, driving across town to woo a tiger.

When he rang her doorbell, a low rumble of thunder rolled across the blue-gray sky. On the tail end of the ominous sound, she opened the door and stared at him like a regal, sable cat. She didn't seem surprised to see him at her door, looking like a starving dog.

"Bella, let's talk."

"Did you come for my jewelry? You can't possibly have any good reason to be here."

"Get your purse. We're going out to the county line and getting married."

She yawned and waved negligently over her shoulder as she walked away from the door. "Go home, John. I need to catch up on my sleep after being out all night for the past two nights."

She looked sensational, small and voluptuous at the same time. Some kind of white, shimmery material was draped around her hips and knotted under her belly button like a low-slung gun belt. The top she wore hung off her shoulders and barely skimmed her naked midriff. He was stunned by her blinding sensuality.

"Listen to me." He followed her and caught her arm in a firm grip. "I don't care about your social life. I don't think you understand what being poor is all about."

That caught her attention. She opened her eyes and studied him speculatively for a moment before smiling. That worried him. It was the smile of puss got the cream, and he'd seen it too often not to be concerned. She sank down onto a white silk brocade couch and patted the cushion beside her.

"Sit."

"No. We don't have time to waste." He glanced at her bare feet and admired the two toe rings and ankle bracelet she wore. The sparkle of her gold adornments made him remember who he was talking to and the fact he was about to do something completely crazy. He had gone completely loco. He didn't want to get married, especially to Bella. If she refused to go along with him right then he was running like hell. "Okay, lady. Listen good and get this straight. You'll never hear me say this again, not to you."

Her pouty lips parted to reveal white teeth and her left cheek dimpled a little. "My God, John. You aren't going to propose, are you?"

Holy Hell. How did she know? He must be slobbering. He grabbed at his pride as it drifted by. "Nothing of the sort. It's a business arrangement." He tried to swallow without her hearing the scrape as it went down. "Well? Yes or no?"

"Is this to help me or you?"

"It's to keep you out of my pocket whenever you want to pay your rent."

"Will we be having sex?"

"Not unless you just have to have it."

He didn't like the secretive smile on her rose pink lips.

"Will you take care of me and buy me food and candy?"

"Don't be a bitch."

He couldn't help the flood of relief that hit him when she laughed and jumped to her feet.

"I'll get my shoes."

* * * *

The Justice of the Peace Chapel was overrun with couples in a hurry to put on the ball and chain. John eyed the group with mild curiosity. He touched the license in his back pocket, glad it had been no trouble to obtain from a friendly judge in Dallas. Bella stood close to him, clutching the bouquet of daisies he had bought for her from a street corner vendor. She poked her small nose deep into the flowers every once in a while and now she had yellow flower dust on her nose and chin.

He wasn't ashamed of the male pride swelling his chest and squeezing his gut. There was no contest as to who had the best looking woman in the room. She hadn't changed her clothes for the wedding. Maybe her bridal garb was a bit unorthodox, but she was a knockout. She had fashioned her mop of sun streaked honey-brown hair into one of those forties looking haystacks on top of her head.

He grinned at her, almost passing out when she smiled at him and ducked her chin as if she was shy with him. He wondered if he would survive six months of steel hard-ons and no way to relieve himself. In a few minutes he would be committing himself to hell on earth. He had to be nuts.

"What are you so nervous about?" She leaned against him, obviously tired of standing in line and oblivious that she was the sexiest woman in Texas. She glanced up at him and he looked at his watch.

"We might be here for days at this rate. Hell, we should have flown to Las Vegas."

"So you're anxious to strap on the old saddle."

He put his arm around her waist and pulled her close. "Watch that kind of talk or I'll strap you on."

Her throaty laugh that was probably meant to cool his blood torched it like she had thrown kerosene on him. Why the hell was she being so damn docile? Cute even? Well, no time to unwrap that mystery now. The Justice of the Peace's assistant was calling out their number.

The ceremony was brief and sobering. Hearing the promise to love and be a good wife coming from Bella rocked him to his shoe soles. He said all the right things without stumbling, but his voice had shaken miserably.

The Justice pronounced them man and wife and it was over. John caught Bella's waist in a light hug, and leaned down, intending to place a chaste little kiss on her parted lips, but she slipped her tongue in his mouth.

The floor dropped from under his feet and the earth flipped onto its side and spun while she pressed into him and moved her hips seductively against his hard-on. He staggered under her assault. The sweet satin taste of her lips and tongue were making him weak as mush. He broke the kiss and dug in his back pocket for his wallet, taking out money to pay the Justice of the Peace. He gazed at her and understood the depth of what he had committed himself to. What laid behind her soft smile and demurely lowered lashes? He'd seen her wind Roman around her little finger with smiles, tears and trickery. *Well, sister, I'm not your grandpa.*

* * * *

It was an omen. The moment he opened the door to leave the wedding chapel, rain poured and lightning flashed. John grabbed Bella's hand to pull her across the parking lot toward his old olive-drab Jeep. That was stupid, of course. In his haste to commit himself to six months of adventure with this unpredictable woman, he'd left the canvas top off and rain was pooling in the seats.

"Let's go in the motel office and take a room to wait this out." He thought it had been a sensible suggestion, but her gaze frosted him over. "What? What's wrong?"

"If you think I am having sex with you in this place, the Blissful Moment Motel, you've lost your mind."

"I haven't made a move on you yet, Bella. I just want to get out of the rain."

She worked her shoulders as if sloughing off something undesirable and huffed. "Okay."

"Okay, what?"

"Okay, I want to get out of the rain, too. I want to leave as soon as this blows over. It's starting to hail! Damn it!"

That was his cue. He picked her up and ran for the cheery looking motel. Tiny blinking lights bordered the large window of the office and when he got the door open, the scent of coffee made his mouth water.

The woman behind the counter eyed them with a smile. "Need a room with a hot bath and some coffee? The coffee is on the house from the machine out by the door."

After letting Bella down, John wiped rainwater from his face and grinned at the desk clerk. "Yes to all that, especially the coffee."

He signed the register and took the key. Their room was at the far end of the building and he wanted to get somewhere to relax the kinks in his back. Funny how he had momentarily forgotten why he was standing there dripping wet, cold, nervous and hungry.

Bella.

A discarded newspaper caught his eye and he picked it up to hold over her head. "Let's go, honey."

He found out she could run like a deer. They reached their humble abode in a flash and she stood hugging herself and shivering while he fumbled with the door key. *Okay, man. You've been alone with Flower many times. Calm down. Nothing different here.*

He silently begged for divine help and as if in answer to his plea, the door opened. She peered around the door as if it were a dark, unexplored cave.

"Your bridal suite, my love." His patience was thinning and he was married to a woman that found him slightly below repulsive.

"What a dump." Obviously too wet and uncomfortable to fight, she went on in and began to take off that postage stamp sized shirt that clung to her like a peach skin.

"Bella, what am I here? A tree stump?" His complaint was halfhearted.

She glanced at him over her shoulder and shrugged. "Stop looking at me if it bothers you. Why don't you get something hot to drink? If I end up with the flu, I'll make your life miserable."

He yanked a quilt off the narrow bed and tossed it to her. "You can stop the strip tease if it's for my benefit. It's not working."

"You're right. If I want to turn you on, I need to go stand on the street corner."

"I'll go get you something hot. Think ten minutes will be long enough?" He really wanted to stay and watch her peel that getup off her luscious body, but he was getting quite a preview through the wet material clinging possessively to her. Her nipples were dark pink and small like spice drops and her pubic hair was dark. The hard drawing in his sac was the signal to beat it.

"I'll be in bed when you get back." Bella was undressing with the aplomb of a stripper, tossing wet articles of clothing toward a chair. "Don't bother me with your racket."

He opened the door and watched her with a grin born of pain from his erection straining to get free. "You just make sure my side of the bed is warm when I get ready to crawl into it."

It was going to be sheer hell. The thing he most dreaded was happening. Bella was lying for him like a cougar and he was the sacrificial goat. He went to the Jeep and found a dry cigar in the glove box and ran for the shelter of the motel office entryway. He lit it and puffed with a sigh of gratitude. At least he had one thing left to enjoy.

Leaning against the motel wall, he contemplated what he had done. *Son of a bitch. You should have gone home to Austin.*

Taking a final puff on the cigar, he went to the coffee machine and got two cups. It looked pretty fresh, but he knew his princess would turn her nose up anyway.

True to her word, she was in bed and letting her naked shoulders show above the quilt. All of her finery was strung out over the furniture to dry.

"Well, you look to be in a better mood now." He handed one of the cups to her.

"I wouldn't count on it."

He sat on the bed and eyed her speculatively, reaching out to pat one of the scrawny pillows. "Move over, doll. I'm coming to bed."

Her movements were deliberate and stiff. "You are not sleeping in this bed." She set her coffee on the nightstand and looked at him through narrowed eyes, but he could see violet fire in their depths.

He didn't know why, but he grinned at her. For one split second, she had looked frightened. That was stupid. Mrs. Cantatore-Lawless was scared of no one. He had no plans or hopes of bunking with the cruel Ms. Bella Flower, yet he couldn't resist pulling the sable cat's tail.

"Well, in that case, can I at least have a pillow and one of those blankets?"

"Help yourself, but don't touch me."

He leaned over her to yank a pillow free and she toppled sideways. He found the edge of a faded green blanket and pulled. It came free from her grip and sailed across the room. She laughed and snuggled down in her comfortable nest, obviously happy to be dry and warm in less than five hundred thread count sheets.

John was grateful she hadn't been up to sexually teasing him anymore that night. She was probably smart to banish him from her bed. There was no way in hell he would have been able to keep his hands off her and he knew she didn't find him worthy of having sex with her.

While he made a pallet on the floor, he eyed his wife who was making soft sounds of contentment. What a fool he was. Sleeping on the floor on his honeymoon. He wasn't a cut steer.

He was hard just looking at her exceptional rear outlined under her blanket. Taking another pillow from the bed, he turned the lights off and settled down on his poor excuse of a cot. He was stinking tired and sick to his stomach. Nerves. She would kill him before his six month sentence was up.

Chapter Three

Maybe Bella had been too mean to him. Sprawled out on the floor on his back in a full royal sleep position, John looked kind of pitiful on that putrid, ratty green blanket with the thin pillow under his head. She looked closer and changed her mind about pity. He was buck naked under that thin blanket and looking as comfortable as a baby in a cradle.

Her inquisitive gaze slowly moved down from his buff chest, over his hard abs and finally to the flat area of his belly. He didn't have a lot of hair on his chest, but the narrow dark arrow of coarse hair on his belly took her gaze straight to the treasure.

Her mouth opened in a soft sigh and her gaze riveted to the lovely, long ridge outlined under his covering. Damn. She checked out his bare feet and smiled in anticipation. At least size thirteen and a half.

Smothering a chuckle, she rolled away from the edge of the bed and thought about what had happened to her. She threw the quilt to the foot of the bed and groaned. Nothing had happened, and probably never would if he still held her in great contempt. *Better look all you want now. He's always been stingy about showing his gorgeous self to you.*

Loving the feeling of being a hussy spy, Bella slid to the edge of the mattress again. She huffed softly at her ridiculous methods of seeing something that by law belonged to her. His private stock.

Carefully catching the edge of the blanket in her fingers, she lifted it. Before she could breathe again, his hand shot out to clamp about her wrist.

"Don't mess with a sleeping shark, Bella." His smile was

disarming and matched his warm voice. "Unless you really want a look-see."

Her heart jumped up and down in her chest while he tugged on her hand. *Hold on to something, fool. He's pulling you off the bed.* "No, no. I was really trying to wake you. You and your dirty mind."

His laugh was quick and rich as Turkish coffee, and he still held her hand. "What's wrong? Your eyes look like big, blue Morning Glories."

Her lips quivered and then pouted in fake bravado. "You're an evil man. You snore and grunt like a pig in your sleep."

"So, you were looking at me, right? Listening, too." His gaze settled on her bare shoulders. "Can I check you out?"

Now, why the hell had she been dumb enough to let him catch her in the unpardonable crime of peeking? She chose a new path. "I don't want to start today with a fight." She eyed his hand that still gripped her wrist. "John?"

He flopped her hand several times, then laughed somewhere deep in his chest. "Yeah, me too. My back hurts too bad to make war."

She froze solid on the bed. He stood and his body rippled in a sun-toasted shimmer of perfectly contoured muscle and sinew.

There was no shame in the man, walking around the room picking up his clothes. He was spectacular, right down to the large scrotum under an awesome length of a half erect penis. He raked at his rumpled hair and stretched. Lord, he was beautiful, and he was grinning at her again.

She drew the sheet up to completely cover her shoulders.

He leaned down to pick up the bedclothes from the floor. She tightened and squeezed her thighs together.

What would he say if she just came out and told him she needed sex? No. Too humiliating if he laughed at her.

"John." Her voice trailed after as she slipped from the bed, wrapped in the sheet. She hurried around the room collecting her clothes from the furniture. "I need to get back to my apartment."

He went into the small bathroom, and then looked around the door at her. "You'll get there, but I think we will be living at my place." She heard the stall door bang shut and then the shower began making clanging and hissing sounds.

He obviously didn't realize he was giving her time to think of a good reason not to do what he wanted. She hit on a good one without too much difficulty. The moment the noise ceased in the bathroom, she stated her position on the matter.

"I'm not living in a place where your girlfriends keep showing up at the door for servicing." She used her most whiney voice to impersonate his guests: "John, honey. Blow up my flat tire. Lube my rear end. Grease my axle. And while you're down there, fill my tank."

He was laughing at her and drying his hair with a dingy looking towel. "Man, I only get half as much tail as you seem to think."

He had put on his worn Levi's that cradled his nice plumbing. She couldn't help it if his smile did crazy things to her, things she didn't want to feel. "Stop bragging and get out of the bathroom." She stared at the washed out green tile and cringed. John stood behind her, and his voice played with her ears and lips until she wanted to swoon like a fool.

"Bella, I'll help you move anything you want to my quarters. We are staying in my place." He hung the towel on the rusty towel bar as if they were raw recruits in the Naval Academy. "I have plenty of room and my home office is set up the way I like it."

"Very noble. Now, have you seen my panties?"

"Not yet." He winked at her and rumpled her hair. "But, I will."

She laughed deep in her throat. "Not likely, unless you do the laundry." She stepped around him to check out the shower stall. "You can't be serious about me showering in there. It's grungy."

"It's old, not dirty."

"Did you clean it?"

"Sure. I swabbed the deck and used a blowtorch on the head."

She stared at him, not certain what he was talking about. "I'll wait until I can use my own facilities."

"Suit yourself."

John left the tiny room to her and she began the distasteful job of washing in the chipped and stained washbasin. She brushed her teeth with a cup of water and a tissue. "Some honeymoon," she grumbled.

"What was that?"

He had radar hearing.

"I said, why don't we just pretend to be living together?"

He came to the bathroom door and stared at her, eyes like chips of green ice. "This can be the longest six months you have ever lived, or be a relatively short vacation. It's up to you."

She couldn't hide the hint of an amused grin. "I didn't know you wanted my company that badly."

He leaned down to pick something up, then handed it to her. "I don't, but that's the way it will be. Uh, your bloomers, ma'am."

"Where were you hiding them?" While she used his comb, John observed her in a quiet, thoughtful manner.

"Say, Bella mia. You go ahead and stay at your place. I kinda hate to give up my privacy. You know, stranger in the house thing."

What was she to do? Why, move right in on top of him, of course. "The arrangement is that we live together. So, we live together." She looked at the floor and huffed. "I'm just not looking forward to it, that's all."

"We'll just go right on to my apartment then."

She frowned, trying to let him know she thought he was a weasel. "I need to go home. There are personal hygiene items I want. You do know what women's hygiene products are, don't you?" She threw her panties at him, and then realized it had been a dumb move.

He held her underwear in his fist and gazed at the white finery and then held it to his face. "Um, yes, I do remember."

"It figures." She tried to look disgusted by his actions, but couldn't hide her fascination with his obvious pleasure in the scent of her lingerie.

He arched his brows in a show of deep question. "What figures?"

"That you would prefer soiled ones." She held her hand out to receive her garment.

His grin was the essence of evil when he went to her and placed the undies on her head, taking his time to fit the waist down to her ears. "Get em' on sweetheart, and let's hit the road."

* * * *

The first half of the ride back to Dallas was fast and quiet. John drove like he couldn't wait to be somewhere far away from her. He had groaned like a bear when she insisted on leaning against him while he drove. He frowned when she fiddled with the dials on the AM radio.

Tired of harassing him, she sat back in the seat and stared out the window at the blur of scenery. The feeling of being in a goofy dream wouldn't leave. She glanced down at her left hand. That was real enough. Bare of any kind of adornment that said she was married.

"John." She poked his shoulder. "I need a ring."

"I'll get you one."

"When?"

He didn't slow the Jeep or say a word while taking the gold military signet ring from his finger. "Stick your paw up and I'll put this on it."

She hesitated before holding her left hand out to him. He slipped the ring onto her finger and over the knuckle. The band was three sizes too big but she didn't care. He took it from her finger and slipped it onto her thumb.

"Will this do until we get back home?"

"Yes. It's beautiful."

She grinned with delight. This was a special moment. After four years of seeing it on his finger, now she had command over the heavy gold ring. Lifting her hand to admire its design, she darted him a glance of uncertainty.

"I can't wear this."

"Why not?"

"This is your Navy ring. It must mean a great deal to you."

"It does." He gave her a quick smile. "Seems only right my wife would be wearing it now."

"Oh." His wife! God, that rang like silver bells from heaven in her ears. She closed her hand to feel the weighty ring with her fingertips. Her voice broke when she spoke to him. "I'll get you one, too."

He caught her hand and squeezed without looking at her. "No need."

"You don't want one?" The hurt was impossible to keep from her voice.

He seemed to have changed his mind. "Well, sure, but I thought you...well, hell yes. I want one." He laid his hand on her knee with great familiarity. She nearly jumped out of her skin when he gripped her thigh and wobbled her leg several times. "Practicing for when we get home...to my apartment...my bed...sex."

His grin obliterated her dwindling reserve of calm. Oh, God, she couldn't be indifferent to this man. Casting a glance at his profile, she could see he was still smiling over her virginal reaction to his touch. Her legs almost parted of their own volition. He would never let her have a minute's peace from now on. Oh, God. She hoped not.

Chapter Four

They were back in Dallas before John figured out just how much his world had changed. Naturally, they stopped at her place first. Her place. He hadn't noticed before that it looked like a fairy had flown through and spritzed the place with female stuff. Oh, yeah. That's right. He'd been too nervous to see past his nose at the time.

"The woman must really love white," he muttered under his breath, walking around the spacious living room. White carpet, white drapery and white flocked wall coverings. He thumped a white chenille sofa pillow.

"Who keeps this stuff clean?"

Bella appeared at the bedroom door and shrugged. "My cleaning company. Why?"

"No reason." He smiled at her and she went back inside the bedroom. "I don’t have a cleaning company."

"I'll contact mine for you."

"Yes, ma'am."

"What did you say?"

He could’ve sworn he’d mumbled too softly for any human to catch his comment.

Her voice had been so sweet and the question perfectly sincere, he had to react in a gentlemanly manner. "I said, yes, you'll have to do that."

After calling himself a wuss, he made a thorough inspection of the little woman’s dwelling. Genuine old masters’ paintings on the walls and artifacts that no big footed gawky male should ever be allowed to walk within a block of such finery. He strolled to the small den where a teakwood desk sat. It seemed sweet little Bella had a hell of an office herself. He glanced at the nesting of awards and degrees on the wall. Holy hell. She was smart.

"John."

He wheeled around to speak to her, but he was still alone in the room. "What is it?" He probably should call her Flower once in a while to keep her on her toes.

"I think there's beer in the refrigerator, if you like." A hollow thumping followed her comment.

"Okay. I'll find it." He squinted down the hallway. She surely wasn't going to be much longer, was she?

Two hours later, he was stretched out on her white brocade couch, bare footed, holding a bottle of beer and studying the few pictures displayed on a library table. The personal array of photos warranted closer inspection. He stood and went to the table, leaning over to peer at the collection.

That must be Bella as a cute little baby being held by a knockout young woman he figured was her mother. He chuckled when his gaze settled on her in an angelic white, first communion dress. Beside Bella was the lovely woman again and Roman. The handsome young guy looking so proud had to be Roman's son, Bella's father. He frowned a little, realizing he'd never seen a photo of the young Cantatores before.

The pictures became more interesting as she matured. Especially the one of her in a bikini on some beach. He picked the picture up to read the gold lettering at the top, "Spring vacation. Scorpios, Greece." *Ah, the legs on that babe.* Her voice mingled with his warm thoughts.

"I'm finishing up. There are some bags ready to go in the Jeep."

She hadn't made a sound when she entered the room. He felt like a jerk messing with her stuff like a cop. He juggled the picture he'd been holding, and it fell to the floor. He picked it up and turned to grin at her. "Nice gallery."

"Thanks." She tilted her head and gestured to the photo. "Don't worry. I'm not taking those."

"Well, hell, Bella. There's plenty of room for them." He gestured to the display. "Are these your parents?"

"Yes." Her expression revealed nothing of her feelings as she carefully took the picture from his hand and replaced it on the table.

"That's it?"

"What do you want? A brass band?"

Her expression was unreadable, nothing he had seen before. "Just curious. Nice family."

"Okay. I don't want to talk about this again. Ever."

John opened his mouth to respond, but thought better of it. Her lips were compressed tight against her teeth and her dark lashes only half veiled the sadness in her eyes.

"Right."

John was concerned by Bella's obvious and up until now, well-hidden trauma over her parents, but he wasn't going to play shrink. All he knew about the young Cantatores was they had died in a plane crash. He had enough ghosts of his own screwing up his life.

But he wasn't down so much he couldn't admire the way Bella looked in the navy short shorts and tiny white cotton pullover she wore. To lighten the mood, he tried to tease her.

"I hope you don't sleep in the raw, lady."

"Why do you care?"

He knew not to push any further. She was in a bad mood and he, of course, was the reason. *Be cool, my man. Just get her moved out of here and into your palatial place.*

"Just looking out for your welfare, ma'am."

His remark went unanswered as she walked back to the bedroom, leaving a wisp of her lovely scent behind. Lord, the smell of lily of the valley and musk rose always surrounded her.

He wondered if she dabbed it everywhere.

* * * *

John's home was nothing like she had expected. There were no beanbag chairs and no nudie posters on the cream walls. No stale beer smell and no gigantic stereo system taking up half the room.

Instead, the carpet was the color of sand, and clean. Tossed against the comfortable looking chocolate colored sofa were half a dozen large pillows. Other women had used those pillows for only Lord knew what. From nowhere, jealousy whipped around her like barbed wire. She picked at the edge of one of the pillows and compressed her lips. John studied her with a wry smile.

"What, Flower?"

"Nothing."

He shrugged and went to the hallway and waited for her to follow. She assumed he was steering her to a bedroom.

She went into what he had called her quarters and looked around. She checked out the closet, then the chest of drawers and a small dresser. No chaise lounge in sight, and the queen bed was covered with an ugly brown comforter. It was going in the trash.

"Don't like my taste, huh?" John asked.

"This isn't taste. It's a nightmare." She walked around the bed and inspected the plain cocoa colored, basic quality sheets. "I could never sleep on these."

He dropped several duffle bags and an overstuffed suit case in the middle of the floor. "Now, why am I not surprised?" His scowl revealed some exasperation. "We can go back for sheets if we must, but it will have to be tomorrow. You can pick up your car then as well."

Bella shrugged and stepped over the baggage to walk out into the hallway. "Where are the linen closets? I will try to make do for tonight."

"Closets? Plural?"

"Yes." Her gaze settled on his lips while she waited for his answer.

"Damn it, Bella." He handed her his keys. "Go get your damn

stuff. I have some calls to make."

She worked up a bewitching hint of tears and gazed into his eyes. "But, wouldn't it be more wifely if I stayed here and put my things away?"

He exhaled as if it hurt and hooked his finger in the waist band of her shorts, pulling her close to press his forehead to hers. "Don't sack the place or burn it down while I'm gone. Now, what is it exactly you want me to bring back?"

She recited a list that made him groan. "Bring a half dozen sets of sheets and two blankets along with my down comforter, a quilt and six pillows." She tapped her lips and added, "And my blue, fuzzy, house slippers."

"What are those things?" He pointed to a pair of feather-trimmed mules she had tossed on the floor.

"Oh, those aren't my favorites." She grinned and picked them up. "I didn't really mean to bring these." With that, she tucked them into his hands.

He looked at her in disbelief. "I'm not going to ask any more questions. I'll just leave quietly."

"I'll be here when you get back."

His glance over his shoulder didn't express joy at the prospect. Bella followed him to the door and waved goodbye to her brand new husband .

She watched from the window until the Jeep peeled out of the parking area, and then began carrying her belongings to his room. Taking his clothing from the closet wasn't easy. The suits and coats were heavy, and the shoes were all on racks.

By the time she had hung most of his clothing in her closet, she was puffing from exertion, and decided underwear would be easier moved. She began to pull socks and shorts from the drawers.

He was tidy. All of his socks were rolled up in cute little balls and his shorts were folded in squares like his T-shirts. It didn't take long to carry most of his stuff to the other room and toss them willy-nilly into drawers.

Next on her agenda was the nice large bathroom. Scooping up combs, brushes and shaving creams, she ran down the hall to the smaller bathroom to dump the grooming items on the vanity. His nightstand caught her eye and she yanked the drawer open. Smiling to herself, she began clearing out his address book, pens and note pad.

Her fingers closed on a cellophane wrapped box in the back of the drawer. When she pulled it out to make room for her things, her eyes widened. Condoms!

He had a huge supply and had used several. A deep feeling of sadness skittered through her heart. This was their honeymoon and he hadn't even thought about using some with her. She had gotten the man she wanted, but the man didn't want her. He was doing her a favor, like she was a duty, a god darn duty. She would be all right if she could remember that. In the meantime, all was fair in love and war and they sure weren't in love. Taking over his room was all for fun, to get his attention. But now, she was feeling too low to enjoy the hassle that was surely coming.

She was still in his room when John came back, loaded down with her things. After making him ring the bell a dozen times, she finally went to let him in.

"Damn it, Bella. Didn't you hear the door bell?"

"I'm sorry, John. I was so busy." She smiled and ran ahead of him and into his room.

"What's going on?" He was still holding a load of bedding.

She ran to his bed and belly flopped onto the firm mattress. "I'm confiscating this room as mine."

He turned around and walked out of the bedroom. She heard him walk down the hall several times and make a couple of trips out to the Jeep. He was obviously carrying her things to that tiny room.

Then he was back, standing at the foot of the bed. He glanced at the open door of the closet, then at the box of condoms on his nightstand.

"Okay. Get off that bed."

She leaned back and clasped her hands behind her head. "No. I'm staying put. I need the room. You don't have anything but an exceptionally large supply of rubbers."

He reached out and caught her foot to drag her to the foot of the bed and leaned over her. "Didn't I ask you to not sack the place?" He grabbed her around the waist and lifted her off the bed. "Back to your own bunk like a good little girl."

She struggled, not to escape but to get him to hold her tighter. He was so warm and strong. "You aren't big enough to make me give it up." She laughed and wiggled, and it all seemed to whet his appetite for play.

He growled like a tiger and turned her in his arms to toss her onto his shoulder, then patted her rear, rubbing as he walked. "Never tell me that, woman. And you are not taking my room. Period."

She wished he would never let her go. Being in his arms made her world seem completely secure. The warm and fuzzy feeling evaporated when he let her down and patted the top of her head. The overpowering urge to irk him took hold.

"Not that I care, but I did notice you chose super small in the condom line."

His movement was too smooth and quick to stir the air as he snaked out his hand and caught her wrist. "Listen to me, Bella. Let's get this straight right now." His gaze was intense as he looked her in the eye. "Until yesterday, I did exactly what every single guy does. Drink beer, watch a few games, date a little. Nothing record breaking, but I was single."

Damn, she couldn't help it. Her chin threatened to quiver. "You're trying to tell me you're sorry to have to give that up? Aren't you?"

"I'm only giving up one of those things."

She wet her lips and sniffed. "Which one?"

He chuckled and hugged her neck. "The games of course." His smile glinted wickedly. "You're my wife for the next six months. If I'm nothing else, Bella, I'm faithful."

Chapter Five

"Want the last of the coffee?" John poised the carafe over Bella's cup. This was the first time she had been in his kitchen and she sure made the place look good. He'd never noticed the way the sun streamed in through the window to touch her. Bella added class to his Spartan surroundings.

"Don't have time, but thanks." She flashed him a quick, kind of sleepy smile.

He hadn't slept much, remembering her little display of meanness and territorial grab over the bedrooms. No matter what she did, Bella was impossible to ignore or stay angry with. Dread ate at his gut. Dread of being alone in the apartment after she left on her trip to New York.

"Bella. Call me tonight, okay?"

She was running through the apartment like a quail chick looking for its mother. She paused long enough to look his way. "What did you say?"

On her next trip passed him, John reached out and hooked his arm around her small waist. "Call me tonight. I'll want to know if you got to New York okay." He arched his brow at her.

"I will."

He couldn't say anything while her gaze played hopscotch over his face and landed sweetly on his mouth. It was as if she had cupped his crotch in her soft, warm hand. "Need cash?"

"Nope." She left him sitting at the counter and made a final run through the place. Outside, the waiting airport shuttle bus blared its horn.

To John, she looked different, dressed in a pearl-gray mini skirt and matching single button jacket. He wondered if that thigh high mini would cover her ass if she leaned over. He hazarded a guess she wore no blouse under her jacket. It was confirmed after he caught a look at one luscious breast when she leaned over him to pick up her handbag. Damn, she was hot.

"John, I'm ready." She smiled and tilted her head to one side like she always did when working on his resistance. "Want to walk me outside?"

"Sure." He held his hand out. "Let me have your gear." He took the bag and followed her outside where she turned to face him. He managed to sound only mildly concerned, not broken up like his gut said he was. "So, when are you coming back home?"

Her perfume kissed his nose and settled in his brain. She gave him a slight shrug and grinned as only Bella could.

"Two days." She started to walk away, but turned back to look up at him. "Will you miss me?"

Damn. What was wrong with him? This was Bella, the brat. Bella, who had gotten him into several fistfights, ran him ragged and tempted him with her sweet curves and smile beyond the limits of any man's imagination. *Be cool man. It's not real.* He smiled at her.

"Like crazy," he murmured. "The driver's watching. You should kiss me."

He stopped any protest she might have had, pulling her close to cover her mouth in a deep, hard kiss. He was expecting sweet, but this was bubbling honey filling his mouth, delicious perfumed exotic desire. Her arms went around his waist and squeezed hard until the shuttle driver honked the horn to break them apart.

She laughed and fussed with her hair. "Think that satisfied him?"

John took her hand. "I don't know about him, but it sure as hell satisfied me."

He put Bella in the van and waved to her as the van drove away. Now, what the hell was so hard about that? He was on his own again, just the way he liked it. No one to worry about but himself. No noise from her CD player. No snack junk on the counter.

He went back inside the apartment and was immediately hit with the silence, just like it had always been. Well, hell. He didn't like it. It had taken twenty-four hours for Bella to rearrange his life. Had she said two days? He wasn't sure he wanted her being on a field trip with a bunch of horny clowns. The crew she worked with was all young and probably better able to talk to her than him. She was from a completely different world than his.

He rinsed out the coffee pot and cups, leaving them in the sink. After watching the morning news, he decided to get the rest of his underwear from Bella's room before going to the downtown office.

When he opened the bedroom door, he stopped in his tracks, the scent of her rushed to him, the scent that always surrounded her. Soft, seductive musk rose and lily of the valley, sensuous yet sweet and tender.

His gaze roamed over the hastily straightened bed and lingered on the delicate white nighty draped over the headboard. *Stop the leering crap. Get your skivvies and get out.*

He walked away from her bed to the overflowing chest of drawers. Pulling out the top one produced six pairs of his socks and several pairs of boxers. Yep, mixed right in there with her lacy bras. Curiosity gripped him in its talons. The satin label in his fingers said thirty-two B cup. Whatever. She had a damn fine set of melons.

He grimaced at his desire to know everything about her, grabbing anything that looked like his. In his haste to vacate her room, he dumped what looked like mail onto the floor. Some of it was torn open, some of it still sealed.

Checks tumbled out of an envelope and spurted in all directions, along with what looked like a bank statement. He grinned as he picked the papers up, figuring he would have to pad her account. It wasn't his intent to pry, but the statement opened and his gaze narrowed as he read the numbers.

Fifty six thousand plus change in checking. Son of a bitch. The accompanying savings account statement reported a paltry four million dollars and change. There were unopened statement envelopes from the Cantatore Brokerage Firm as well. Son of a bitch!

Forcing himself to remain calm, John got out of her room and dressed for work, wondering how the hell he was going to carry on sensible conversations with clients while his head was spinning with the knowledge he was her fool.

The phone rang and he was pulled from drowning in a pool back to familiar ground.

Checking the caller ID, he spoke into the mouthpiece. "Hello, Mom. How's Dad?"

The conversation was of general things. He should tell his mother she had a brand new daughter-in-law. No. Not yet. He'd wait until the fair Bella was with him. Let her explain for herself. It would be a lot more fun.

* * * *

The cloying, warm air of the Victorian mansion added to Bella's state of agitation. Normally, she was eager to work assignments and this one was a peach. It was a renowned mansion in upper New York, four stories, overflowing with antiquities from all corners of the world.

She couldn't think of anything but John. John and his kiss that had shattered all her former ideas of what she felt for him. She was in love and always would be. With her husband. Her fingers caressed the wide gold band of his Navy ring. No, her wedding ring. She had wrapped tape around the band to keep it on her thumb. It kept him close and she couldn't wait to call him that evening.

"Bella."

It was the company's latest hire, a nice looking blonde guy.

"We're going out for drinks this evening. Want to join us?"

She shook her head and sighed. "Not tonight."

Not tonight or ever again. Last week, maybe. Last month, she would have been the first to walk in the club's door. But, that was before John became her man.

The day wore on and she kept a constant eye on the time. Bella took notes and made comments on the musty old mansion's furnishings, but her thoughts were back in Dallas, occupied with six-foot three inches of warm male. She shivered and wrote her married name in her ledger for practice.

Looking around at the rather common items, Bella wondered why the agency had put her on such a minor expedition. The stately old Victorian house was filled with antiquities from all over the world, but she wanted relics. One particular relic that was never far from her thoughts was the set of ancient ceremonial wedding goblets given to her parents while they traveled in Scotland. They were hundreds of years old and had been used by royalty in their lavish marriage celebrations.

Roman had a letter they had written in their excitement over the gift and their eagerness to get back to Dallas, but thieves had robbed them while they were out of their room and took the goblets.

The goblets were deeply important to her, becoming her quest to find the relics. She attached great meaning to that piece of history, something her parents had loved enough to want to bring home with them. But, they hadn't come back. She had been left with nothing but memories and money. Until now.

Bella was elated when the work detail wrapped up for the day and everyone headed for the hotel.

She went straight to the phone the second the door to her room was locked. Her heart thumped while she punched in the numbers John had written in her day planner. His phone rang, but his answering machine took the call.

"This is John. Can't catch your call right now."

Then the usual salutation. Her voice wavered when she spoke in to the mouthpiece after the beep. "I guess I have the wrong number."

Where was he? He'd asked her to call him. Her hand shook and she dropped the receiver. Loneliness was not a new emotion to Bella. But it was worse when fear and pain piled on, too.

She despised herself for it, but she called him four more times. After eleven o'clock, she accepted defeat. Before the sting of humiliation could dig in too deep, she realized his big old kiss had been a joke. He just gave the little gal a cheap thrill. So much for fun and not having any.

She was in New York and the night was young.

Chapter Six

Their argument had begun quickly, sharp words accompanied by her glare of disdain. John picked up Bella's luggage and walked beside his uncommunicative wife through the noisy Dallas airport terminal.

"Where were you last night and the night before?" He held onto her arm and squeezed. "Is it too much for you to keep your panties on for twenty-four hours?"

"I was out, having a good time." Her teeth showed in a bare grimace. "Does that piss you off?"

"Damn right." He noticed her eyes were red rimmed and her lips were chapped. "Listen, Bella. I don't like the idea you have that I'm some kind of house boy in your service." He swung her tote bag up on his shoulder and scowled at her. "I ask you to do one civil, simple thing like call in and you can't bring yourself to do even that. You're thoughtless and a bitch to deal with most of the time."

"Stop the husbandly ownership thing." She shook his hand off. "Maybe I got tired of waiting for you to answer your phone."

"Try again, Flower. As far as I can tell, you didn't spend either night in your room."

"Don't try that on me. You were the one that was out. You whoremonger."

His lips quirked in amusement. "Whoremonger? And, Mrs. Lawless, what do I call you?"

"Single. I'm going back to my apartment."

"Okay." He wondered if she really would move out of his place. But, hell, if she did, his life would be a lot saner. "I'll help you pack."

She iced him for the remainder of the ride home and pushed him away when he tried to help her up the steps to the apartment. She rushed inside and threw her bag and briefcase onto the kitchen table.

"I'll be out of here tomorrow."

"Fine." He opened the refrigerator and took out a bottle of beer. "I can't wait." He eyed her while taking a long swig.

"Stop looking at me, and don't talk to me." Her voice shook on the last two words.

He bowed in a courtly manner and swept his hand out toward her to emphasize his intent of being no barrier to her leaving.

"And don't you dare touch me."

"Have I ever?"

She compressed her lips and stared at him in silent anger. He crossed his arms over his chest and studied his wife. Why was she pissed at him? He knew she didn't give a rat's ass where he was, what he did or who he did it with. And why the hell was he so steamed at her? He was ticked at himself for the display of jealousy and she was right. It had sounded like an inquisition. He watched her take a breakfast bar off the counter.

"Are you hungry?" he asked.

"No."

"Then put the bar back."

"Kiss my ass."

How many times had she suggested he do that? Just every time he ruffled her tail feathers. The awful truth was, he loved the way she said it with that soft little drawl on the end. It always sounded more like she was asking a question. He was one torn up bastard. Treating her like she had rules to follow. What rules? *Man, you should have gone home to Austin.*

He killed the rest of the evening finishing up some paperwork and looking down the hall toward Bella's door. After one o'clock, he gave up. He couldn't concentrate knowing she was angry and hurt. He went to her door and knocked lightly.

"Bella?" Silence greeted him. "I'm turning in. Want to talk?"

Something plunked against the other side of the door. He was sure he could hear her crying. "Bella?"

He wanted to comfort her, to make her stop crying. Every time she cried over something he had said or done to her it had always ripped him to shreds. Before, he could walk away from her and not hear her sniffling and sobs. That had all changed and he was supposed to reassure her and hold her. Not make her cry.

"Bella."

Something crashed against the door and he heard her muffled response. "Leave me alone."

Obviously, the more he tried to appease her, the more upset she became. Heaving a rough sigh, he went to his room, leaving the door open. Sleep wouldn't come. Ordinary house noises were magnified because he listened so intently for any sounds from her. The hall clock chimed like Big Ben. Three o'clock in the damn morning. He punched his pillows and rolled onto his back, groaning in disgusted misery.

He opened his eyes to find Bella standing beside his bed. He must have dozed off for her to be able to come in his room undetected. He barely caught her whisper.

"John."

"You okay?" He reached for her hand. "What is it?"

"I didn't do what you think." She made a sniffling sound and rubbed her eyes. "But you did."

He propped himself up on his elbow, considering her accusation and pulled her down to sit on the edge of the bed. "I'm a bastard." He caressed her back.

"Do you believe me?"

"Yes, I do. It wasn't my plan to keep you under surveillance, Bella." He inhaled roughly. "I just wanted to know you were okay."

She wiped her eyes again. "Where were you?"

"Riding my Indian out to the ranch and on down the highway. By the time I got back, it was too late to call you and explain." Unable to tell her how he had really felt, he bypassed revealing his shredded dignity. He cupped her chin in his fingers. "Where were you?"

"In the hotel lobby. I just sat there like a fool until the bar closed and security asked if I was a guest."

John groaned and touched her cheek. "I was stupid for questioning you. Forgive me for being a pig?" He could see her nodding her head and heard her sniffle again. He chuckled and patted her leg. "Want to crawl in here with me?"

The deep silence worried him for a second. Then he heard her soft laugh.

"Goodnight, John." She stood and walked out of his room.

He couldn't resist. "Hey, this marriage would go a whole lot better with a little sex."

"I'm sure it would be little, too."

He was still grinning at her insult when he went to sleep.

* * * *

The next day began with no sign of pending trouble. John was up before his alarm went off at five AM. Bella was still asleep, so he left her a little love note on the counter, stating he would be hungry when he got home. He laughed out loud at his humor, figuring his bride didn't know a stove from a washing machine.

At mid-morning, John left his office in the Cantatore building to call Max. It amazed and kind of provoked him that the man feigned surprise at the sudden wedding. The first thing Max wanted to see was the marriage license, which John handed to him with a grin. He reclaimed it as soon as it had been photocopied and duly recorded.

"John, my boy. I'll buy lunch and you can tell me how you're going to get Bella to sit in on one board meeting once a month." Max chuckled and got his hat.

"That is none of my affair, Max. I plan on spending a lot more time at the ranch from now on. What she does is her business."

"Roman wanted her to come into the business with him. Is she still set on looking at old junk?" Max smiled at John as if he were hatching a new plot.

"Her work is important to her." John opened the door and walked out into the broiling Dallas heat.

Max shook his head. "Never understood that myself. She was wild about them."

They walked in quiet camaraderie toward a nearby steak house. Once they were in the cool interior, they ordered a beer and discussed everything but why Bella refused to speak of her childhood. John figured that was an area best left alone.

"So, John, you know Roman would be pleased as punch with this wedding." Max sipped his beer. "Yes, sir. Pleased as punch."

"You think so?" John smiled at his companion.

"Indeed, he would be." Max tapped the tabletop. "Any wars been fought at the Lawless abode?"

"A few." John thought about the loud quarrel that had erupted between them the night before. "We get along pretty well." He remembered the pounding on the adjoining wall of his neighbor's apartment because of their loud horsing around.

"I'm glad to hear it." Max looked at his watch. "How did your folks take the news?"

John laughed. "They don't know."

"I know they'll be pleased. Bella is a fine young woman."

John choked on his mouthful of beer. That was what he had never got through his head. Bella was only twenty-one, but gave the impression of being a much more experienced woman on the outside. A very spoiled, sexy woman.

"John?"

"Sorry, Max. Just lost in thought." He found himself extremely anxious to be with his wife. "Just wondering what's for dinner tonight."

By the time he got home, the sun was setting and he was hungry. Seven o'clock and no aroma of pot-roast calling him to the kitchen. No rattle of pot lids signaling a man-pleasing meal was being prepared. John chuckled over the ridiculous expectations and went into the living room.

His loving wife sat on the floor with a bowl of something in her hand, spooning whatever it was into her luscious mouth.

"What's for dinner?" He almost choked on the comedic question.

She waved the spoon around and didn't look up from the game show she was watching on the television. "Ice cream and blackberries."

"Now, Mrs. Lawless," he squatted down to smile at her, "that's not a meal to keep your husband satisfied."

"If you want something else, cook it."

He stayed where he was, eyeing her like a hungry hound while those sweet, plump lips sucked on blackberries and cream. This was one cruel woman, giving him an inkling of how artful her lips could be, how quick her pink tongue lapped out. Without thinking, he grabbed her hand and took the bowl from her. He couldn't take anymore of the licking thing.

She still had the spoon in her hand. "I'm not hungry."

"You're not, but I am."

She jerked her hand from his grasp, splattering ice cream over the front of his navy-blue shirt. He eyed her with a crooked grin. "Baby wants to play?"

The soft chortle from her throat went double time to his crotch like an unexpected caress. To cover his immediate needs, he dipped his fingers into the bowl and smeared ice cream on her lips and chin.

She jutted her chin out and pointed to her lips. "Now, clean it off."

Her demand was met and his heart went on a rampage of flip flops and high jumps while he cupped her chin in his hand and licked a path over it to her lips with a leisurely sweep of his tongue. He couldn't stop the tremble in his hands or the desire to taste her parted lips.

So this was bliss. Soft, plump, satin bliss led him down the path to his basest desires, telling him to suck her lips into his mouth and slip his tongue deep into the warmth he had longed for.

How sweet and smooth and cool with vanilla ice cream. Her sweet mouth beneath his seemed to be responding, softening and yielding. There was no mistaking the slide of her tongue against his, or the exploring of his mouth with quick darting swirls of tasting, pulling in and out, like a hummingbird. She was leading him to the edge and pushing him over and Lord, he wanted to free fall.

He pulled back, taking the spoon from her hand, his voice husky with emotion. "Let's go."

"Where?" She drew back and wiped her chin. "I'm not hungry."

He reached down to pull her to her feet and gazed into her eyes. "Okay. You have a choice. Cook or make reservations somewhere."

He let her go when the phone jangled in a jealous intrusion and he grabbed the noisy contraption. It was his ranch manager's girlfriend.

"Yeah, Ellie." He walked into the kitchen, pulling his tie off and unbuttoning his splattered shirt. He wrote on a note pad while he talked to the Ellie. "I'll come out as soon as I can get away."

He turned around to find Bella staring at him with a dark glower.

"Going out?"

"Not exactly out." He could swear she was jealous, but Flower probably had no idea what jealousy felt like. "That was Ellie. There's some kind of emergency out at the ranch."

"What?" Bella's eye's narrowed as if she was suspicious of his reason to be leaving the apartment.

"There's a problem in the stable. They thought I might want to be there." He lifted his shoulders in a broad shrug and pulled his shirt from his pants while Bella followed after him.

"Can't it wait until tomorrow?"

She still held the spoon in her hand and John thought about the sweet softness of her mouth. "She said it was urgent." In a way, he was glad of the excuse to get away from the teasing minx. "Got a colicky mare."

"Can I go with you?" She went into the kitchen to put her dirty dishes in the sink. "I'm not working tomorrow."

"You hate Ellie. And you'll be whining to come home before I get everything done." He went into his bedroom and pulled a long sleeved chambray shirt from the closet. "Remember last Fourth of July?"

Bella looked away as if she were in complete disgust at his audacity of ever bringing up the event. "That was a friendly disagreement."

He patted her rear as he passed behind her. "I'd hate to see a declared war between the two of you."

She stood quietly and observed him while he traded his slacks for some comfy faded Levi's. "You really don't want me to go with you?"

He turned around to look at her, tucking his shirt down in his jeans. "I'll be back in the morning."

Her voice was soft, emphasized by the flashes of sapphire fire in her eyes. "John, if you spend the night with any woman, it's going to be me."

Her statement caused his crotch to tighten. Yeah, it was the oddest feeling, but Bella could touch his cock with a word or a smile or gesture. She had just done that and he began to firm up.

"Bella, baby." Maybe if he made it sound disgusting, she wouldn't insist on going. "Okay. You can help vaccinate the colts and castrate a stallion. But not until we watch our prize mare being bred."

"You wait right here, Mr. Cowboy." She hurried off toward her room, turning to look at him.

"I'm waiting right here, Flower." He grinned and sat down to wait on his impulsive and beautiful wife. He did want her to go, but damn, she was not the rancher type. Sure, she could ride a horse, but she didn't know where steak or chicken nuggets came from.

Heavy thumping sounds came from her room and he smiled to himself. "You okay, Bella?" He looked at his watch. "I have to get going."

She didn't answer, making him curious about what she was doing. He was standing up when she trotted into the living room. He fell back in the chair to stare at his evil seductress. One glance at her outfit rocked him back on his heels.

She was something a man dreams up when he is at his most horny and deprived. Lush, hot and gorgeous. She set a CD player on the coffee table and turned it on, full volume.

The music was pure barroom scene, hot and nasty.

She stiffened her shoulders and pumped her hips in time with the throbbing beat. Like a bug to headlights, his gaze clamped on the snow white, butter soft looking chaps she wore. That was it, except her lacey white see-through demi bra. Just the chaps over a sheer, white thong barely covering her crotch.

She rotated her lovely hips and turned her backside to his full view. He swallowed the long mournful wolf howl in his throat. Her butt was naked, flushed a toasty pink, looking a lot like a couple of delicious creamy bon-bons.

Damn. He wasn't sure his heart was still beating, and was sure he'd gone into a mild cardiac arrest when Bella began her cheerleader routine. It beat the hell out of anything he'd seen at football games.

She swung her ass from side to side, doing a shimmy so fine her breasts jiggled like a belly dancer's while her lacy demi bra slipped lower. He'd been in every kind of strip joint, bar and dance club and they all paled in Bella's company.

She was setting him on fire and he wasn't about to stop the show. Why would he? It had been a long dry spell since a woman had entertained him and she was doing it so well. No doubt about it, Bella was one hot tomato and he wanted to roll her, mess up her hair and leave a love bite or two on her lovely throat.

He was hard as cobalt. Hell, she kept his cock on alert most of the time and it occurred to him she was having too much fun making him miserable.

He stood. "Bella." She was a born Delilah. "Cut it out."

His direct order only seemed to whip her in to a laughing frenzy of swiveling hips and thrusting titties. Her buns were glistening with some kind of shimmer and her naked back glistened with a mist of perspiration from her workout.

Like a fool, he yelled at her. "I'm telling you to stand down."

"Why?"

To his dismay, she ran to the CD player and cranked it up a notch and proceeded to bunny hop with her hips bumping out toward him. He'd had all he could stand. His mouth watered to taste her sweet bouncing breasts and his tongue was hard from want of licking the cleft between her legs. He made a lunge for her, but she scampered off to the terrace and smiled while he lay sprawled on the floor.

Seconds later, he was on his feet and stalking after her. She was like a greyhound, cornering with skill and darting to and fro, jumping from couch to chair and over the coffee table.

"Get ready, Flower." Who was he kidding? He could hardly run with such a hard-on.

When she ran out onto the terrace, he was thankful. She was winded too, but stood defiantly grinning at him.

He had no idea how much noise they were making, but at that moment he was pretty sure it sounded like in a riot in their apartment. He cornered her and she screamed, picking up a plastic lounge chair to throw at him. He tried to wrestle the chair from her and discovered she was a lot stronger than he had guessed.

"Enough now, Bella. You're finished."

"Kiss my butt, John."

"I plan to."

He watched in helpless amusement when she swung the chair behind her and over the terrace wall. It made a hell of a clatter on its way down to the pool garden.

They stared at each other until the doorbell chimed. Several times. He pointed his finger at her. "That's trouble and you brought it."

He walked to the door, turning the music off on his way, taking a second to rake his hair with his hands. This could only be a pissed neighbor. Nope. A pissed off apartment manager. She was petite with piercing black eyes that looked into a renter's soul.

"Mrs. Wells." He tried charm. "How nice."

"Don't bother with the nice guy thing this time. Your friend and you have had your last party. You are no longer welcome here." She took a long, scornful look around his male comfort living room.

"It was the chair, wasn't it?" He would have tried to look pitiful, but there was Bella in her thong.

"Among other things." The biting comment was accompanied by her look of disgust in Bella's direction.

"What if I apologize to everyone in the building and pay for the chair?"

"No. Do you happen to recall the terms of your lease? The little talk we had when you moved in?" The stern woman in charge glanced sharply at Bella. "Noise was number one."

"I apologize. We just got carried away."

"I would prefer you find another place to party by the first of the month, if you can't make it any sooner."

"First of the month it is, Mrs. Wells."

"Fine. I'm counting the hours."

The petite, gray-haired, motherly looking woman strode away like a peacock. John shut the door and turned to find Bella peering at him like a guilty pup.

"Okay, you. Start packing."

"Are you mad?"

"What do you think?" He nailed her with a dark glower. "I've lived here three years without any trouble. You live here three days and we are told other living arrangements would be appreciated." He advanced toward her and she had the balls to laugh.

"This means we move into my apartment."

"The hell it does. This means we move out to the ranch. We need the room anyway. And with all the screaming you do, we need to give other people a break."

She tried to run past him but he caught her by the waistband of her chaps.

"John, stop it. I'll scream."

He laughed and raised and lowered her a couple of times like a shopping bag. "Go ahead. You've done all the damage you can do for one night."

Her shrill scream ripped through the apartment and he lowered her back to the floor. He grimaced when the doorbell began to ring again.

She pointed toward the door. "John, the door."

"Screw it." He wiped sweat from his brow.

"It's the manager wanting you out tonight."

He glared at her. "Me?" He shook his head and went to the door, opening it, prepared to see Mrs. Wells.

"Look, Bella. It's Mom and Dad."

Chapter Seven

Bella read pure disapproval on Mary Lawless' face as she took quick inventory of the situation. Mary barely tolerated her and now here she was being naughty with Mary's precious only son. Bad Bella. His mother's keen observation swept over Bella's scanty get-up.

"Well, my goodness. John and Bella."

Emphasis on 'and Bella'

The pregnant pause sucked the joy from the air and Bella was awash with indecision.

What to do? Act like a shy little girl caught playing doctor or be herself. John skinned his shirt off and wrapped it around her shoulders, grabbing at the tails to hide her panties.

"Mom and Dad. What a nice surprise."

The CD player still blasted in the background and John hurried to shut it down, and then returned to Bella's side.

Still smiling, Mary arched her brows. "How nice to find you here too, Bella."

"Hello, Mary." With a serene smile on her lips, Bella hugged John's waist, not offering further explanation for her presence. Her big, strong husband could do that.

"Hello, Bella. It's a pleasure to see you again." Hall was always a gentleman and Bella did like him. "You two kids had dinner yet? Mary and I are on our way home to Austin and just decided to barge in on John."

She wanted to hug the man, but thought better of it because of her garb. "Well, honestly, Hall, we haven't had dinner, but John says he has to go out to the ranch."

Squinting at his son, Hall frowned. "What could be more important than taking care of a guest in your home, son?"

Bella smiled up at John, enjoying his expression of discomfort. "Actually, Dad. Bella's not a guest."

She imagined Mary's backbone rising like a cornered cat's and Bella was set for fur to fly.

"Not a guest?" Mary's smile froze on her genteel features. She gazed at Bella with rounded eyes.

John spoke up, making the situation crystal clear. "This is Bella's home. We're married. She's my wife."

Bella was stunned by the mix of emotions charging through her. Surprise and devotion toward John for claiming her as his wife, stepping up to face his family. The air sizzled with tension, but she didn't worry. Bella stood where she was, waiting for the explosion of angry rebuke from John's parents.

His father was first to break the uneasy quiet.

"Married? Why, that's wonderful." He hugged Bella and shook John's hand, patting him on the back. "We couldn't be more pleased."

A new sound filled the room. Laughter. Mary Lawless embraced her new daughter-in-law and shed tears.

"When did you get married?" Mary dabbed a handkerchief to her eyes.

John looked nervous. "Three days ago."

"Three days ago." Hall shook John's hand and continued to question his son. "Where in the world did you have the ceremony?"

"The Justice of the Peace outside Paris." John took Bella's hand and drew her arm around his waist.

Mary almost sobbed aloud as she gazed at the young couple. "Justice of the Peace? I wish you would have included us. I wanted to have a beautiful wedding for my only child."

"Mom, Dad, I'm sorry I didn't let you know."

Mary reached out to touch Bella's lightning struck looking hair for the first time. "You must have been a beautiful bride, dear."

Bella's heart fluttered a little. She saw hurt and confusion on the woman's face and she had caused it. "Mary, we simply fell in love and it just happened out of the blue. John asked me to marry him and I would have been a fool to say no."

Bella gave John a crooked grin, figuring Mary's tears were from disappointment. The immediate crises seemed to have passed and after a few minutes, she slipped away to her bedroom to change her clothes. She looked up when John came into the room. She was in her panties and a bra that hung open in the back.

"Been some evening, hasn't it?" He touched her hair and laughed. "Evicted and busted by the folks in less than an hour. You sure bring new meaning to putting a little fun in your life."

"Right. Now your mother has a reason to hate me."

"I think she took the news pretty well."

"She probably thinks I'm pregnant."

He shrugged and winked at her. "She wants to be a grandmother someday."

John took time to call the ranch and inform his manager he wouldn't be there until the next morning. Bella wasn't taking credit for the delay. He could have left anytime he wanted.

She moved away from him and began to fashion her long hair into a French braid. "As long as those kiddies aren't from 'Bad Bella.'"

He lifted his hands and groaned softly. "We won't go there right now."

"With all the company arriving, we never will." She turned around and waited for him to fasten her bra.

He traced the curve of her neck with his fingertip and whispered against her cheek while closing her bra. "Let's just worry about getting through tonight." He didn't leave the room, but watched her dress in azure blue silk lounge pants and a matching sleeveless top. "You look great."

She didn't want him to see how deeply his compliment affected her. "You don't have to say nice things to me, John. I'll be good while your parents are here."

He caught her shoulders in his hands and gazed into her eyes. "I never say anything I don't mean."

Her heart pumped madly and her eyes were misty. "I won't forget you said that."

* * * *

Dinner went smoothly enough. John sat beside Bella and occasionally touched her hand, probably for his parents' benefit. She caught him smiling at her several times in a way that had nothing to do with humor. He was probably thinking about her impromptu hoochy-koochy dance and how she had gotten him thrown out of the apartment he liked.

"Bella." John's mother spoke to her. "You and John will have to spend some time with us in Austin."

The woman had gone out of her way to exclude her from any family gatherings, and sent Christmas gifts to her apartment instead of inviting her to accompany John to their home. Bella winced at the half hearted invitation from her new mother-in-law.

After glancing at her husband, Bella laughed. He looked worried about what her answer would be. "I doubt that will be possible anytime soon. I'll be traveling a great deal for the next few weeks. Who knows what will happen six months from now."

John's glance was sharp and questioning. "Traveling? To where?"

His obvious resentment filled her with a strange feeling, a mixture of power and regret. She didn't want to go anywhere he wouldn't be.

"Well, yes, dear. My job. I've been assigned to Mexico and on to Seville if our lead doesn't furnish enough information."

His eyes narrowed. "Oh, yeah, your job."

Mary seemed to sense the abrupt cooling of emotions between the young couple. "I think it's wonderful you have a career." Her face flushed and she picked at the tablecloth. "I have to say it—you and

John, married. I'm still in shock."

"No more than me." Bella met John's gaze and laughed. "I mean, I'm shocked that John wants me." She knew Mary disliked her. Oh yes, the reasons were varied. Public notice describing her frequent speeding tickets and releasing chickens from their crates on hot loading docks.

Probably the worst infraction had been calling for him to help her out of a jam on Christmas Eve two years ago. She couldn't shake an amorous date that had wanted more than she'd been willing to give. Of course, she called John. It was his job, but he had been at his parents' home. Before the incident, Mary had been cool, but ever since that incident, she had been frosty.

The touch of his hand on her knee beneath the table was thrilling and disconcerting. He leaned over to kiss her cheek and murmured against her ear. "We're going to talk about these trips when we get home."

Her gaze touched his with soft promise of pleasure she wanted to bestow on him. Why did she do it, think about releasing the wild passion that had been building for four years on him? No, he wasn't interested, not when he had a life away from her that was sane. He was with his real family and she was the intruder. She was his duty, not his passion.

To hide her bruised feelings, Bella caught John's hand weaving her fingers through his. Touching him eased her worried heart.

The quiet evening evaporated as soon as John's parents left for Austin and the newlyweds closed the apartment door for the night. Bella kicked her shoes off and stomped down the hall toward her room.

"Why do you care now about what I do?" She threw her blouse in his direction.

"Why don't you make a list of the dates and places you'll be off saving an old moldy book or bedpan?"

"So, that's what you think of my job." She unzipped her slacks and scowled at John. "You don't really care where I am."

"Okay. So I'm having a hard time not keeping an eye on you. I still worry about your safety. Kind of territorial, huh?"

"Kind of? You sound positively testosteronial."

"That's not a word." He leaned against the doorframe and watched her brush her teeth.

"Bella Flower, someday we are going to sit down and share our best kept secrets."

She breathed deeply to calm her nerves. What was he talking about? There were secrets she would never share with him. No matter how much she loved him. Her hand shook when she rinsed her glass and placed it on the vanity.

"John, you only enlisted for six months." Her heart ballooned in her chest and stopped beating. "You don't have to stay with me for the whole tour of duty if you don't want to."

The crackling of cold silence shrilled in her ears and her lower lip developed a bubbling, crazy pulse. John's face, with its angles and tanned handsome planes, blurred as her eyes filled with tears. Silently cursing herself, she struggled to keep the tears from escaping down her cheeks. His gaze narrowed and she couldn't tell if it was humor or fire in his green eyes.

"Not stay with you?" He drew his finger up the satin lapel of her robe and smiled a lazy tiger smile. "You're too anxious to be rid of me."

She moistened her lips. "You're reading things into my statement."

"Statement? I think it was a challenge." He toyed with a wispy curl at her temple. "I accept."

Mustering up a look of scorn, she yawned and moved away from him. "Just so you understand, I will not be responsible for your whining later on."

* * * *

She made sure he remembered his station as her temporary husband and her secrets were hers to never tell and damned if she didn't have lots of them. Nothing about Bella was his to love or keep. The little arctic cat was never going to thaw for him, never look at him with yearning, or touch him just to feel his presence.

Her behavior puzzled him. She said the right things and smiled when she should, but he always sensed she was pulling away from him. And her earlier dirty dance routine had been nothing but a cock tease. She was an enigma.

But, he hadn't been wrong in thinking there had been desire in her eyes at the same time she told him to watch his ass if he stayed with her. Right now, she was curled up on the couch with a quart of ice cream and laughing at a sitcom designed for less sophisticated tastes.

She glanced up to smile at him and set the ice cream carton on the end table. Did she do things like that to piss him off? Sure she did. Her apartment was pristine, so he would ignore her attempt to make him yell at her. He would much rather watch her snuggle down in the same brown pillows she had scorned in the beginning. *God, help me remain sane while she's in my life.*

"John." She took a legal pad and pen on her lap and scribbled something on it. "I'm making a list of all the places I will be when I'm on assignment." She brushed at her curly hair and wrote with a serious scowl on her face. Then she tore the page off the pad and held it out to him. "I really won't be given that many assignments. I'm too new and haven't had time to prove to them that I'm trustworthy."

Her smile was sweet. He got up to take the sheet of paper and glanced at it. Where were his legs that could run ten miles with no trouble? One little gesture of civility from her cut them off at the knees.

"This is really thoughtful of you, Bella." He sat down beside her and pretended to study her artful scrawl. After placing the sheet of paper on the coffee table, he gestured toward the ice cream carton. "I'll finish that."

She handed him the carton and her smile set him off on a wild trip of sensations. Strange things happened to his gut, like little feet running across his spleen and tap dancing up his spine. God. He was in love. In love and totally pitiful. The lady was far above him, and when she deigned to speak to him, her voice was lyrical.

"There are more blackberries in the refrigerator."

He chuckled. "No thanks. This is fine." The frozen confection sharpened his desire to suck on her lips. Lord. They were the most alluring things he'd ever seen. Soft, plump and slightly parted, then open when she laughed.

"Bella." He dropped the spoon in the empty carton. "I'm heading to my bunk."

She hugged one of his revolting pillows to her breasts. "So early?" Her lashes lowered like a butterfly in motion.

"I plan on making some phone calls from my room." He picked up the paper she had given him and smiled at her. "Have you forgotten we have arrangements to make before the first of the month? Moving vans and boring stuff like that." Her look of cool distain amused him. "Don't worry your pretty little head, Flower. I'll handle it."

She nodded, yawned and patted his thigh. "Good thing because I have a lot to do."

"Really?"

"Well, yes. A ton of research for my next assignment and a new agent to train."

"What about shopping for chow? If this diet goes on much longer I'll have to seek medical help. I'm about to starve to death."

She bunched her shoulders and rolled her eyes. "I'll go shopping tomorrow evening. Maybe."

John eyed her, never taking serious for one second her plan to shop. But he was curious about what had caused her resistance and outright lack of concern with anything connected to home and family care. Draping his arm around her neck, he jostled her playfully.

"Don't you care if your cupboards are bare and your laundry is piling up in the utility room?"

"Nope." She moved a fraction and slapped at his hand that teased her earlobe.

"What did your mother tell you about the way to a man's heart?"

Bella's personality changed as if hit by a whirlwind. "She didn't tell me anything." Her eyes narrowed and her mouth settled into a deep grimace. "I don't want you to mention her again."

He tried to hug her, but she lay back and drew her legs up, hiding her bare feet under a pillow.

"Bella, I'm sorry." He caught her arms and pulled her onto his lap. "I forgot. Okay?"

Her eyes rained reproach at his audacity. "Don't you dare pry into my life. It's nothing to you."

"Your life?" He laughed. "Well, lady. Right now, you are my life."

Chapter Eight

The big, yellow moving van arrived at the first of the month and carted away the furniture from John's apartment. Bella had packed her things and was ready to move into the house at John's horse ranch outside Dallas. She liked the place with its colts and fragrant stables and small creek to wade in. But she didn't want to become too fond of him or his home, so she kept her feelings to herself.

The one skunk in Eden was Ellie. Everything about the woman irritated Bella. Most importantly, Ellie was far too familiar with John. Laughing at his jokes when they weren't funny, giving him a tonsillectomy kiss at the New Years Eve party last year, pretending to be shy when she was as bold as brass bull's balls, and touching him at every opportunity. "Well, honey. That stops as of today."

John looked around the kitchen door. "Did you say something, babe?"

His pet names were coming more frequently and his frown less often. If she didn't know him better, Bella would have sworn he kind of liked having her around. Of course, she had made the effort to be less destructive of their relationship and his reputation.

"No, I was singing." She smiled at her handsome husband and mentally sent a hot kiss to his wonderful mouth. "John, we will be the only ones living in the house, won't we?"

He came into the kitchen, carrying a large cardboard box. "Sure. Only other person will be Ellie while she cleans and cooks. But she goes home to Buck's at night."

Bella carefully wrapped tissue around a water glass and thought over her next comment. "She doesn't need to clean. I can do that." The worry in her heart won out and she lied to him. "I really can cook you know."

The sound John made was a cross between a choke and a snort. "Bella mia. No way." He caught her hand and pulled her close. "I know you don't care for Ellie, but sweet thing, she stays to do the cooking and cleaning."

No problem, Bella assured her ego. Ms. Ellie would be put in her place. "Okay."

John rubbed her back and kissed her cheek. "Fine. Now, let's make a sweep of the place one more time." He began checking the cabinets and pantry. "You finished in your bedroom? I saw a box on the floor."

"Oh, that." She didn't want to talk about packing while she contemplated gaining residency in his bedroom for the next few months with no strings attached, but he was waiting for an answer. "I put it in my car."

He looked around and raised his brow with a wry grin. "Looks like it's time to go. We've done all the damage we can do here." He jingled the door keys. "I'll lock up and turn these in to Mrs. Wells. I'll meet you at the ranch."

The look on his face was pure regret and she was to blame. Bella felt a tug of guilt tighten in her stomach.

"I'll see you in a little while then?"

He followed her out of the door and touched her hair. "Yeah. Be careful on the highway."

Bella got into her car and drove off toward John's place, stopping at a gas station for a soda before getting on the highway. With the CD player off and the window down, she could hear the wind and occasional birdcall. The whistle of a Bobwhite sounded sweet in the evening air and strangely made her anxious to see John.

Her sentimentality made her a little nervous. Don't get goofy over him now. This is not your first date with a guy that thinks you're hot. He is doing his job. With a burst of new resolve to simply survive the coming weeks, she turned sharply off the highway onto a peaceful dirt roadway. The aroma of grass and sunshine was indescribably delicious. She rounded a curve in the roadway and experienced a jolt of pleasure when she saw the ranch house.

The serenity of the place touched her heart, making her glad she had not made a fuss about living there. The sweep of the low-slung roof of gray slate over white stucco was breathtaking. Enormous oaks and cottonwoods stood overlooking the place in silent splendor. The split rail fencing held up a wild scramble of red and white roses that scented the warm evening air.

"My God, how beautiful." Her comment drifted off in the warm air as she got out of the car and walked up the pathway to the double front doors. A blur of black and white ran around her and Bella laughed. Roscoe, the small collie that belonged to Buck and Ellie had come out to greet her. She patted his head and walked up to the front door. A turn of the doorknob and she was inside the cozy house.

"Welcome."

Bella flinched at the sound of the twangy voice. "Ellie." It was obvious the young woman hadn't expected her to be part of the bargain when John moved in permanently. "Which is John's room?"

That felt good. Bella inclined her head toward the cool looking hallway.

After Ellie found her voice, she chattered like a magpie. "It's right down the hall, the big one with the beautiful view of the creek." She raced ahead of Bella to open the door at the end of the hall as if it was a special honor. "John didn't tell me you were coming to spend the night."

"That's okay, Ellie. He doesn't know yet." The shocked glaze in Ellie's eyes fortified Bella's desire to taunt the interloper.

Ellie stood in the door observing the brazen newcomer. "Here it is. Can I show you where things are?"

Bella breezed past the housekeeper. "No, I'll let John handle that."

Punching her signature of ownership home, Bella dropped the tote bag onto John's bed.

The bloated pause was wonderful to Bella's way of thinking. She had shocked Ms. Ellie. "By the way, I would prefer you didn't clean in this area of the house anymore. Personal reasons, you understand."

"I see. Okay, then. I'll be in the kitchen if you need anything, Bella." She smiled and Bella compared it to the stare of a hungry boa constrictor waiting to devour her man. Ellie inhaled in apparent tension before she hurried off to the other side of the house.

Heaving a sigh of contentment, Bella looked around. So this was John's room, all twenty by twenty-five feet of oak floors and cream, stucco walls. The large room was bathed in a soft glow coming through double hung windows and wide plantation shuttered doors that opened onto a broad expanse of shady terrace. And the bed—Lord, what a masterpiece. It was high off the floor and wide as the Pecos.

"Hello, heaven." Her whisper was followed by a soft gasp of surprised guilt when she heard the rumble of the Jeep pulling into the circle drive and hurried out of his room to the one she supposed to be hers. Euphoria hit her after she discovered the adjoining door between their rooms.

Locking her hands behind her back, she turned to face John when he tapped on her door.

"Like it?" His gaze went to the sheer broom skirt that revealed her slender form thanks to the light pouring in behind her. "Did Ellie show you around?"

"I don't need her. You seem to forget I spent a few weekends out here with you and Roman." She walked across the floor to look out the terrace doors. "Want me to help you unpack?"

He looked doubtful. "You have enough to handle. I'll probably wind up helping you stow your skivvies away. I'll whistle if I need you." He was still in the room and still holding the bag. The warmth of his lingering gaze made her breasts swell and her nipples pucker. His footsteps were directly behind her. "This stuff found the wrong room again." He leaned forward to rest his chin on her shoulder.

She didn't turn around when she answered him. "Oh, my goodness." In her most coy way, she laid the blame elsewhere. "That must have been Ellie's mistake. Just leave it there."

The air was drenched with incredible aromas, roses and spice and essence of male. She shivered when he pressed against her.

"Did you want to stay in my room?" He brushed the sensitive skin of her neck with his lips.

He most assuredly could smell her desire for him. And why not when she had become moist and hungry? She felt like a slinky jaguar, playing with her potential mate. Her sidelong gaze was meant to fire his hormones into action.

"You must earn my favors."

"Name it."

"You're too willing."

His grimace was followed by a groan. "That's a real understatement."

Her lashes fluttered prettily. "How long has it been, sailor?"

His husky reply pleased her. "Too damn long."

"Have you forgotten how?"

"I think I could manage to thrill you, Flower."

White heat flared between her legs and their strength had vanished. He was sex talking her. With her legs all but gone, she had to lean against him, get closer to his steely erection. The heat of it burned through her sheer skirt and sent thrills up her spine. She twisted around to taste passion fruit but gall filled her mouth.

Ellie was standing in the doorway, staring at them.

"I don't want to be a bother, John, but supper is ready. Do you want me to stay and serve?"

Bella was certain the blond bombshell had been spying and had broken in to ruin their love play on purpose. She tried to sound friendly while speaking to Ellie. It was damn hard. "We can feed ourselves."

John gripped Bella's arm and tried to atone for her abrupt dismissal of the housekeeper. "Thanks, Ellie. We can handle it from here."

Ellie's face glowed. "Okay, John. If you're sure."

"He's sure." Bella was smiling but her nails dug into his ass.

John caught Bella's hand and walked her toward the kitchen. "I don't have to know why you dislike Ellie so much, but would it be too hard to treat her like a human for the next few months?"

His words didn't sit well with Bella. She forced his arm away and frosted him with her gaze. "Easy as pie, if she stays in her part of the house."

* * * *

John couldn't remember ever seeing a more desirable woman anywhere in the world. Bella the beautiful, his wife and companion. He grinned at her when she looked up to meet his lingering gaze.

"How's the chicken?" Hell. It must have suited her fine. She was on her third piece and a second helping of mashed potatoes and gravy.

"It's okay." Bella licked her lips and reached for a fragrant roll. "What did she make for dessert?"

John finished his iced tea and glanced at the buffet. "Looks like blackberry cobbler."

"I hope there's ice cream."

"Anything for my lady." John got up to find the ice cream and get the cobbler. "You're in luck."

Bella got up to look in the refrigerator. "I don't see any Italian ham or wedding cookies." She made a face at the lima beans that were being soaked for the next day's meal. "I'm going down to the stream." She widened her eyes and gestured toward the table. "Unless you want me to help clean up here."

"As a matter of fact, I do." He handed her a platter. "I have a lot of work to catch up on and I don't have a lot of time."

He saw rebellion flare in her blue eyes, but she bit her lip and took the dish. "Okay, I do know how to clean a kitchen."

"Kind of sorry you were rude to Ellie, are you?"

"Shut up." Bella dumped the scraps into the disposal and tuned the water on. She worked quietly until he smacked her butt in a little love tap and grinned at her. She bumped him with her hip and laughed.

"Ms. Bella." He knew he was courting danger but forged ahead. "Is that a signal that you're ready for my attention?"

For a moment, the expression in her eyes was indescribably beautiful, soft as a blue cloud carrying earth-shattering passion ready to rain down on him.

"You again, sailor?" She shook her rear at him and went back to her task. "I don't start work until later tonight. Look for me in the room above the saloon."

John was hard just being close to her, feeling weak and horny most of the time was wearing him out. In the past few weeks, Bella had proven to be a mind-boggling distraction. She made herself so available but never invited him to partake of her bounty. She never hid her lush body from him, but never shook it in his face either.

This was a first for him. Being in the same quarters with a desirable woman and keeping his ideas and hands to himself. What was wrong with him? Bella was his wife. He wanted sex with her. He wanted to sleep all night with her. His case of the horns was embarrassing. He must have left his balls in Pensacola.

He jumped like a guilty fool when the phone rang. Any diversion was acceptable at the moment.

He grabbed the receiver. "Yeah, Buck. This is John."

He couldn't understand the dirty look Bella shot his way. He shrugged and gave her a questioning look. She turned her back. "Yeah, I'm still here. Okay. I'll be right out." He put the phone down and reached for her hand. "Are you pissed?"

Her expression was a doozey of a mixture of anger and seduction. What the hell? The woman knew how to screw with his head.

"Want to go out to the stable with me? You like Buck, don't you?"

She sauntered to the refrigerator and pulled out a bottle of wine. She smiled at him over her shoulder. "I like Buck, but I wasn't planning on spending the night with him."

What did she say? Hell fire. Coming from Bella, that could mean go to hell or take me. He was just plain afraid to come right out and tell her what he wanted.

He inhaled roughly. "I won't be gone long. Just have to check in some supplies that arrived today."

"That's okay, sailor." Her gaze drifted over him as if he were her every desire. "I'm going down to the creek to cool off."

"No, don't do that. I'll be right back." He pushed the screen door open, and then changed his mind. He must be nuts. "To hell with the supplies."

He reached for her but she evaded him.

"Don't let me keep you from your mare." She grinned and poured some wine in a paper cup. "I'm really too tired to wade in the creek. I'll be in my bedroom."

He didn't move until she left the kitchen. Whatever she was up to couldn't be for his benefit. Damn it. He slapped his thigh in disgust. That was it. The end. They had to start communicating, and they would. The minute he figured out her language.

Chapter Nine

The inventory that Buck had surprised John with seemed to be taking one hell of a long time. Buck was dragging his feet and taking too many breaks. He looked at his watch. It was eleven o'clock. Damn it. John tossed his dry ballpoint pen aside and grabbed a pencil. The tip was broken off.

"Are we about finished here, Buck?"

His foreman was busy counting sacks of sorghum and oats. Man, why had he ordered so much?

"You in a hurry to get back to the house, or something?" Buck grinned at him.

"Yeah, or something." Keeping his mind on horse feed was impossible when all he could think about was the possibility that Bella was stretched out on his bed, nude. Ready and eager. "Let's finish up here, okay?"

Buck shook his head and took the clipboard from John's hand. "You go ahead. Doesn't seem like you want to be out here at all."

John clapped the insightful man on the back and laughed. "Don't want to offend you, Buck. But, I have something on my mind."

He forced himself to walk with a little dignity instead of sprinting out the stable door. Pausing a few yards from the barn, he gulped in fresh air. In contrast to the rich soup of aromas in the stable, the air outside was thin and clean.

He rolled his tense shoulders for a minute, stopping abruptly when a worrisome thought hit him. He probably had it all wrong, and his little Bella Flower had been playing with him as usual.

How many times had she accidentally placed her hand between

his legs and squeezed his privates while she crawled over him to get in the car? She'd even dared to look at him with innocent blue eyes.

What the hell? He had to find out. He might just wake her up and find out what she had on her mind. His step slowed when the sweet scent of musk roses teased his nose, the source coming from the heavy loaded vines on the rail fence. The fragrance reinforced his desire to wake Bella for an all night session of hot sex. Maybe she could be softened up with a scarlet rose.

He snapped a lush bloom from it and sniffed its perfume as he hurried to be with his Flower.

Gravel crunched beneath his boots and the kitchen screen door squeaked as he went inside the house. Damn. He was on his way to ruining the moment.

He tried to be stealthy, but bumped into a small table in the dark hallway. The table's legs squalled like a cougar on the flagstone flooring as it slid away to finally bang into the wall.

His heart stopped, and then resumed beating like thunder in his chest. He exhaled in defeat. No use trying to make a sophisticated entrance now. He wanted to shower before cajoling, or teasing, or just plain begging Bella for her sweet loving.

His room was completely dark and he needed time for his eyes adjust to the pitch. A minimal amount of light tumbled in through the open terrace door. Okay. Time for that shower if he could find it. Hanging the rose behind his ear, he reached for the shower door, but instead froze to the spot where he stood.

"Don't shower, sailor." Bella stood looking like a shimmering moonbeam in a white nightgown.

"I want to taste you, not soap."

The soft purr of seduction had come from her lips, the goddess standing near the terrace door. John made his first open move on her, walking slowly to where the shimmering Venus waited.

"Funny, I was thinking the same thing about you."

She stepped closer to him, lifting her arms to his shoulders. "So, you have always wanted to see me naked?"

"More than anything." His voice wasn't his own in its husky timbre.

He couldn't believe it. Her arms were trembling. His baby was as nervous as he was. Going slow was another form of torture, but he was trying hard to be a man and let her dictate the action. He was ready to simply lift her gown and be inside her, no questions asked.

Instead, he slipped his arms about her slender waist and held her close, not daring to squeeze like he wanted to.

"And you've always wanted to make me cry out in pleasure?" Her voice broke in the middle of her provocative question.

"Affirmative."

He remembered to take the rose from behind his ear and settled it in the silky depths of her hair.

He reveled in her soft sigh.

"Then get ready," she murmured, hugging his neck. "I'm about to break the sound barrier."

He'd foolishly believed making love to Bella for the first time would be the source of a thunderstorm and the sound of breaking windows. Oh, no. This was nothing like that. This was perfume and tremors of emotions so deep he would drown if it got any better.

* * * *

She sighed as he kissed her, equaling his passion, her soft lips parting to murmur delicious words like, "touch me, love me."

She said the things he had longed to hear, her sultry voice stroking his libido with a silken finger. No longer able to restrain himself, he gave in to the whirlwind of passion and let his desire go free. Cradling the woman who had been his only desire for so long was unbearable in its pleasure. His body ached for her and his heart tumbled off into space, leaving behind a shell ablaze with raw need.

Her curvaceous body pressed into his, warm and yielding, making him forget his thoughts of being cautious.

"Bella," he groaned, not sure what he would say to her.

"Yes, darling." She clamped her fingers deep in his hair and bit his lip.

When she drew her leg up to press tightly against his thigh, John held her close and sampled the sweet silky interior of her mouth. His breathing was painful and ragged, but he couldn't let go of his treasure.

He could breathe later, when the storm of passion had subsided.

He moaned with gratitude to be holding a wealth of priceless booty and he had all night to explore it. He loved the way she placed her hand over his, working her fingers between his, all the while moving her hips against him in a sensuous undulating tease.

Her mouth closed over his and her tongue probed and darted and licked to tantalize him into a semi dream state. His sex was too rigid to be held captive much longer.

She made soft little sounds that only an aroused woman pursuing completion made. The power of all his denied urges swamped over John as he pressed her to the wall to gain better leverage. In the filtered moonlight, he could see her looking up at him with her most wicked smile, standing perfectly still while he pushed her gown's soft straps off her shoulders and down her arms.

The filmy material fell to her waist and his throat squeezed shut. Her breasts were delicious looking with small nipples that looked like cherry candy. He couldn't help it, couldn't stop the sound coming from his throat that sounded like something a cave man would emit.

Deep, rough and pained.

She took pity on him and lifted her arms up to cling to his neck. "Does that mean you like me, John?"

He pulled her roughly to his body and kissed her hungrily, touching her with hands that couldn't get enough and filling his cup with the taste of her lips. She was every sensation and sensual dream he had ever experienced all packaged into one gorgeous woman.

He lifted his head and gazed at the beauty in his arms. He wanted to see her eyes and drown in their blue depths. Her breath played with the spot on his neck she had sensitized earlier with her playful nipping. When she spoke to him, he shivered with desire.

"I feel something really big and hard against my leg." She moved her hand down to press against his belly, but went no further. "Is that your spear?"

Damn. She was still bent on driving him nuts. He caught her hand and pressed it to his throbbing erection.

"No, baby. That's my torpedo." His loud groan echoed around the room and filled his ears while she gripped him in her hand, alternately squeezing his erection and tracing the engorged veins with her fingertips. "Careful, Flower. It's primed to go off."

She laughed provocatively and pressed against him, laying a path of kisses on his neck and chin. His hands felt clumsy when he pushed her gown over her hips and caught her waist to hold her between his legs. He was going to come if she didn't stop bucking her mons up against his member.

As if she read his thoughts, she unbuttoned his shirt and pushed it back to lick his pecs. While he was shaking with need, she unbuttoned his Levis and slipped her hand in his boxers. She could never have imagined the flame that shot through his blood when her fingers gripped him and moved back and forth along his length.

"Baby." He released her long enough to skin his clothes off and kick them aside. "I want to make you yell with happiness."

He picked her up and carried her to his bed, placing her in the center of the enormous piece of furniture. He was completely enamored of her, beside himself with need. But she looked at him with such sweet desire. He would hear her yell before the night was through.

She lay back, watching him with a soft smile. "If you want a light, I don't mind." She let her fingertips trail over her flat belly then touched his lips. "No light is fine, too."

John could barely work the switch on the bedside lamp. When light bathed the room, he saw a work of art with a devilish smile in his bed. She was propped on pillows, her smile telling him she had no plan to leave him that night.

"Bella, my beautiful Bella." He positioned himself over her and kissed her mouth, skimming his palm down her belly to her hip. He knew before he touched her she was like silk, sleek and warm.

His member lurched forward to seek out its pleasure, but he held off. He tried to not rush, longed to give her new pleasures, the kind she would never forget.

This was what he had waited for, had wet dreams over. Her legs quivered and he caught her scent of arousal, encouraging him to lick his way to the soft curls that hid an ecstasy. He knelt between her legs, pulling them up over his shoulders.

She slowly pushed her hips upward to his mouth and laughed, the sound sultry and all woman. He licked the soft skin of her inner thighs and opened her with his thumbs, tasting her with a deep thrust of his tongue. Her reaction was instantaneous, tremors of excitement tensing her thighs while he held her firm, licking and probing her delicate folds.

Her bud bloomed and pulsed as her orgasm drew closer. She clawed his arms and gasped, loud and raspy, moaning in her growing frenzy.

At the last moment he caught her bud in his lips and sucked hard, continuing to pleasure her as she cried out in delight, writhing in her climax, reaching the summit three times to his absolute happiness. He gave her everything she wanted and held her until she relaxed against him and laughed softly, holding her arms out to him.

"John, did you hear me call for you?"

"Prettiest sound I ever heard." He moved up to pull her close. "Want to try again?" He was shaking with emotion and concerned he couldn't wait until she gave the okay to charge ahead.

Her lips brushed his and while her tongue slipped in and out of his mouth, his erection became impossible to gauge. He whispered against her ear. "You have any idea where those extra small rubbers are?"

She sat up to look at him and laughed seductively. "Of course." She leaned over him to open his nightstand drawer and pulled out the controversial box of condoms she had found in the apartment. "Think this box will be enough?" She pulled one from the box and tore off the cellophane.

"Let's make a test run and see where we stand."

His abs bunched and jerked in excitement when Bella took him in her hand and slowly rolled the condom onto his ridged sex. She looked so damn sweet and concerned about the perfection of her work that John grabbed her and quickly laid her on her back, settling between her legs in anticipation.

She wasn't shy or afraid. John enjoyed her take-charge way of holding his sac in her palm, squeezing lightly while driving him insane with her deep kisses. Her hips came up to meet his member as he pressed forward with a groan of disbelief. She gripped him so tightly he couldn't pull back. The flesh of his back stung where her nails dug in.

He looked into her face and saw desperate longing and a glow of passion in her eyes. He took his time, stroking her bud with his member, easing her into the heat of climax again, cupping her butt to hold her close. Intense yearning hit and he could no longer resist the climax that held an end to his fiery torment.

His thrusts became deep and powerful, set in rhythm with her arching movement. Her sobbing cry of his name drove him forward, urged him on as he ground his hips against hers, not letting her part from him until his seed was spent and the rivers of fire in his blood were quenched.

He dropped onto her, kissing her each time she sighed, whispering his appreciation in her ear.

She clasped her arms about his waist when he tried to roll from her.

"Don’t leave me yet, John." She nuzzled his neck and sighed, pulling the flattened rose from her hair to place between her legs.

He grinned at her and covered her flower garden with his hand. "I’m not going anywhere, Bella."

Chapter Ten

Bella's laughter bubbled like warm sherry around the kitchen and filled the soft morning air. The room smelled of lovemaking and roses.

"Don't suck so hard. You'll destroy it."

Her instructions to John made him laugh, the rich sound mingled with hers. The moment was so perfect and exciting that Bella teetered on the edge of delirium. She faced John, straddling his thighs as he sat in a straight back chair.

"John." She moaned in obvious distress. "I said not so hard." She shrieked with laughter. "No biting."

Her laugh quieted under his kiss. The cherry popsicle they had been sharing splattered onto the gleaming black and white tile floor.

She hugged his neck and gazed into his eyes, rocking to and fro against his member, smiling as he hardened. A soft gasp teased her throat as he caressed her inner thigh. Like an artful pickpocket, she reached into the warm space between them and squeezed his straining erection.

He inhaled deeply and touched the damp curls between her legs. "I love the way you smell, Flower." His tongue flicked out to taste her bare shoulder. "Just drives me crazy."

His kiss stirred her soul. Bella reeled in the wild concoction of emotions that gripped her as their lips touched. If he knew she had practically fainted during one scorching kiss, he would probably laugh at her. She would never let him know.

The last hours had been stolen from Eden and she wasn't willing to retreat back into their old relationship. Taking several minutes to study his face, Bella sighed. "I think we will do this a lot."

"You know a lot about pleasing a man, Bella." He nibbled her earlobe. "Do you have a specialty? Something you prefer to do?"

There it was, a subtle opening to checking into her sexual background. She leaned back to look him in the eye without resentment or embarrassment. "My pleasure giving depends on how pleasing the man is." Had she shocked him? The glint of green fire heightened in his eyes and she explained her meaning. "John, obviously, you've had more than a few lessons yourself."

He tightened his embrace. "You forget. For years it was everyday routine to grill you." His voice had been gruff.

Bella accepted his pitiful excuse for prying. "Don't ruin it. I won't ask questions if you won't."

He gazed at her in quiet speculation for a moment, and then grinned. "I'll try to stop doing it."

"Good. Then be quiet and kiss me."

"Aye, aye, ma'am."

His kiss began slow and soft before changing into a hard, demanding delight. This was surely something she had dreamed up, her and John, making out in the kitchen at five in the morning. She wanted it to never end, but it was being meanly interrupted. He stood up with no warning and his sudden jostle irritated Bella. She moaned in disappointment.

"What is it?" She couldn't think of anything important enough to cease their pre-dawn lovemaking.

"I forgot about Buck and Ellie." John cupped her rear in his hands, holding her tight as he went to the door and looked out the window. "He's already working in the stable. I'll have to change his schedule."

Bella turned in his arms to peer out into the bleary light. "He won't be coming up here, will he?"

"No, but Ellie will. She starts fixing my—our breakfast in a few minutes."

Resentment stung Bella's heart. Someone always took away the things she loved, but not this time. "I can't believe anyone wants to eat at this time of morning."

John tilted his head to smile at her. "I'm sorry, honey. It's just a routine Ellie has when I'm here. After she gets Buck fed, she comes up here and throws something together for me. I just reheat it and eat whenever I feel like it." Pulling her tighter to his waist, he asked her for the seemingly impossible, "Will you try to get along with her? Maybe you'll even learn to like her?"

Bella snorted and laughed. "Sure." Pressing her face to his chest, she scraped her teeth over his pec before looking into his eyes. "Since our privacy is about to be invaded, carry me back to the bedroom."

"Which one?"

"Ours, of course." She dug her heels in his butt and laughed.

Her laughter trailed behind them as he hurried back to the bedroom and fell onto the bed with her. He grabbed her legs to pull them around his waist, his loud groan expressing pleasure as her fingers guided him to her.

* * * *

They moved with urgency, taking every drop of bliss the moment offered, coming together in a final burst of white-hot heat. She fell into a whisper of a swoon as he sucked her nipples into his mouth and teased them with his tongue.

"Um-um, don't ever forget how to do that, John." She stretched and lounged back to watch him squeeze her breasts in his big hands.

He kissed her stomach and grinned. "Not likely. Tastes too good to forget." He groaned as a noise coming from the back of the house caught his attention and he got up to shut the door.

Her grin was followed by a knowing laugh. "It's a good thing we left the kitchen, honey." She eyed his erection and touched her inner thigh. "I'm glad you don't mind getting naked, John. I love looking at your nice tush."

He leaned over the bed and caught her foot. "You can look at anything I've got." Parting her legs, he smiled lazily. "I don't want you hiding from me."

Pure feminine design commanded her to touch her breasts, and then slide her hand down to touch herself. "Never, John. Never ever."

The moment was right and they had all the time in the world as far as Bella was concerned. She held her arms out and he went to her, covering her with his strong, vital body, filling her and driving her upward to touch the stars. He was her man, her lover. He was a king. He shone like the sun.

Later, after their shower, Bella sat on the edge of his bed slowly massaging lotion over her body, making sure John observed her technique. He shook his head as her hands circled her breasts and slid down to her belly and on around to her hips.

"Do you think I'm soft enough, John?" She stood and smoothed the length of her legs.

He stopped patting aftershave on his face and slipped his arms about her waist. "You're perfect, but I'll never be soft again."

Bella hugged his neck and took a deep breath, tasting and memorizing his scent of sun-warmed sagebrush and lavender. The aroma of a precious spice drifted through the mix, all just enough to make her dizzy with pleasure.

"I could take care of your stiffness right now, John. I don't want you to be in pain." She patted his tight rear.

He grimaced playfully and thumbed her nipple. "Will you put something on? I have to go to work today." He kissed her hard, and then went back to getting dressed.

Bella's heart pounded as she tried something with John she had never achieved before.

Quiet agreement.

"You're right." She hurried through the connecting doorway to the other bedroom. What was he thinking right then, and what should she say next? Would he want her so passionately if she became sedate and demure?

She was filled with dread. She pulled a white silk sheath from the closet and when she spoke to him, there was a hint of a shake in her voice. "I'm going to be busy, too."

She didn't like the lengthy silence before he spoke.

"Anything fun?"

She smiled and wondered what he would think if she said he was the only fun in her life. "Lots of fun. I have a paper to write on an archeological dig in Utah, and I'm going to toss my old clothes."

"Bella, you don't own any old clothes." He gazed at her from the doorway. "Going shopping?"

His expression had taken on a slightly familiar touch of disapproval.

"Yes. I plan to be gone all day and spend lots of money." She quickly pulled the dress over her head and walked to him. "Zip me."

He stopped knotting his tie to help her, dragging his knuckle up the delicate line of her spine. "There's one thing I don't want you to toss."

She turned to look up at him with a soft laugh. "What's that?"

His grin was crooked and sexy and Bella trembled in the pleasure he gave her.

"Your wedding outfit. Okay?" His words infused joy in her heart.

"Okay." The trembling voice she heard couldn't belong to her, but it did. How was she going to squeeze enough pleasure and happiness from the next five months to last for the rest of her life? Having known John for so long, she could tell when he was emotionally involved and just being flirty, and right now he was serious.

This was something new, and she was stunned at the ease her feelings just spilled out at his feet. She didn't care. Throwing her arms around his neck, she stretched up to kiss his mouth hard.

"Nothing will happen to that outfit, John."

He touched her sleep rumpled hair and kissed her nose. "Be careful on the highway today." He kissed the curve of her neck and smiled at her, his question sounding matter of fact. "Do you need money in your checking account?"

She lifted her gaze from his hand to his eyes. What was that glowing in their depths? She wished he would just come out and ask her whatever he was hinting at. After a quick inventory of things she hadn't told him, she was more worried than ever.

Her reprieve came with the slamming of the kitchen screen door. Ellie had come into the house.

"It's just me. Ellie. Here to make breakfast."

For the first time since knowing her, Bella was glad to hear Ellie's twang spinning through the house.

John patted Bella's rear and kissed her again before leaving the bedroom. "Well, do you need money?"

"No, I'm good."

She took in the nice line of his broad shoulders and narrow hips, shivering with the remembered delight of being held in his strong arms. The drop of Pandora blood in her veins wouldn't be denied and she went to his closet to pick up one of the loafers that he seemed to favor. Catching her lip between her teeth, she held the shoe up to the light. Her grin was followed by a chortle. Size thirteen. "Lord, don't I know it."

Bella was still smiling when she slid onto the stool next to John. Their eyes met and he grinned at her, positively surrounding her with desire. She laid her hand on his thigh, patting and exploring while eyeing him with invitation. "Hi there. You work out?"

Before she could blink, he caught her face in his hands and took her lips in a hard, deep kiss. When she slumped against him, John held her up and whispered against her lips. "In case you've forgotten, Flower, I'll be back tonight."

"I'm looking forward to it," she replied, her voice little more than a wispy croak.

She couldn't think of anything but the possibility of dragging him back to their bed and making love until he couldn't walk. Even the way he ate toast and crisp bacon was a sexy act to her. He held a bite of scrambled egg to her lips and she took it in her mouth, chewing with her eyes closed, murmuring over the marvelous taste.

He filled her plate from his and they kissed between bites and laughed when she dropped crumbs down her cleavage. He quickly leaned over to brush them off and then licked his fingers. She sighed and pressed against him until Ellie appeared in the pantry door.

"Good morning, folks. You look chipper this morning." She carried several cantaloupes to the cabinet behind the counter.

Bella couldn't resist taunting the woman she saw as a rival for John's affection. She leaned her shoulder against his arm and looked at Ellie with a smug smile. *Look at me, Ellie. I'm glowing because I had hot, long lasting, climax after climax sex with John.* He put his arm around her waist and ended the bad girl image she had tried to convey.

"Ellie, we were waiting for the best time to tell you that we're married." He patted Bella's hip. "I guess this is the time."

Bella nudged his leg with her foot and pinched his arm. She would have milked the setup for as long as possible.

Ellie smiled brightly and stretched over the counter, offering her hand in congratulations and shook hands with the newlyweds. "That's great." She grinned and went on enthusiastically. "Buck and I decided to tie the knot this Christmas."

Bella drew her hand back and gazed at the woman she held in low esteem, wondering if she had simply been green-eyed jealous. No, Ellie rubbed herself all over John anytime the chance came to her. For now though, Bella would be friendly and remember to keep an eye on Ms. Ellie.

"How nice, Ellie. I hope you will be as happy as we are." A soft choking sound from John made her flush. It worried her. Was he so very unhappy with the deal he had entered into?

He stood and carried his dishes to the sink. "Ladies, it's been nice, but I've got to meet a client in the handball cage."

Bella didn't laugh or smile. His knowing how to play handball was one more thing she never knew about him. She slipped from her chair and went to the door with him.

"Be careful on the highway, John." She smiled up at him. She liked saying intimate, caring things to him. "Hurry home. I'll have something to help you relax."

"Now, Bella." He led her outside to the shady patio. "You don't exactly make me relax."

"You'll have to trust me."

He groaned and caught her up to squeeze her tight, nuzzling her neck. "Stay out of trouble, at least until I get home."

She pressed her hand to his member and sighed. "I don't like it when you say things like that to me." She stepped back and gave him a cool once over.

"Damn it, Bella. Are you pissed again?"

"I'd rather you didn't talk to me like I'm five years old." She spun and took several steps toward the kitchen door. "I'm twenty-one, John." She lifted her chin and glanced back at him over her shoulder. "Go on to work."

She heard his steps as he walked to his Jeep, jumped when he slammed the door and started the engine. He drove off in a screech of tires and flurry of pebbles. She crossed the patio and sat down on the glider. She was heartsick, already missing him and wanting to cry.

The roar of the Jeep's engine made her look up. He was coming fast and sliding around the curve of the driveway. He jumped from the Jeep and came toward her. Without a word, he reached down to pull her from the glider and buried his face in her neck, lifting her up on her toes to kiss her deeply, finally pressing a quick, hard kiss to her mouth.

"I know you're not five years old."

He set her back on the glider and drove off, leaving her to hate herself for being so insecure.

Chapter Eleven

"That's the one."

John tapped the glass display case and smiled at the elderly man waiting on him in the posh jewelry establishment. It was one of those up the stairs places with walnut paneling and burgundy drapes. It also smelled of money. When he rang the bell for admittance, John hadn't been sure he had done the right thing. After all, there were dozens of jewelry places in Dallas, but the elite frequented this one. Only the best was fit for Bella.

The slender, perfectly groomed gentleman took the ring from the case and placed it on a blue velvet cloth. "You have a remarkable eye, young man."

John studied the fine piece of jewelry for several minutes, awed by the color of the four carat round cut stone. "It's for a remarkable lady."

The remark earned him a smile. "A blue diamond of this size and grade is not to be found any longer. The vein this beauty was taken from closed ten years ago."

John shook his head and laughed. "Looks like I got here just in time. I would probably never find a diamond the exact color of her eyes again."

"Indeed, sir." The salesman didn't ask if John wanted the ring. He simply polished it with a jeweler's cloth and put it back in its white silk box. "May we put that on your account, sir?"

"You bet." John dug in his jacket pocket for his wallet. He wasn't sure he had an account in the pricey place, but when he flipped his credit card out onto the counter, the salesman didn't blink an eye and wrote up the deal. No vulgar cash registers here. All deals done on silent paper sales pads. What a place.

"The ring is yours, Mr. Lawless, if you'll sign here, please."

Nodding his head and knowing he must be grinning like a fool, John took possession of Bella's wedding ring. He couldn't wait to put it on her finger. He thought about the lie he'd told her as an excuse to get out of the house early.

Handball. Hell, that sounded like a lie even to him. But, he had wanted to get into Dallas early and get the ring for his little woman.

After he got back to his office, Max dropped by unexpectedly. His nod and pat on the back told John he had definitely done the right thing.

"Bella's a well spoiled female," Max said, settling into one of the club chairs in John's office. "By that I mean she's spoiled in a genteel way that goes with a beautiful woman."

John glanced up from the ring he had been admiring. "I don't suppose you have talked to her about the upcoming board meeting." He took two cigars from the desk humidor, handing one to Max. "I sure the hell am not bringing it up. She hates me enough today as it is."

"Left the house in a hail of dishes, did you?" Max was laughing at John and puffing on his cigar.

"No, just rage." John leaned back in his chair to watch the blue smoke trails collecting on the ceiling. "Not from me. Her."

"Hmm. She's temperamental and easily hurt."

"Don't you mean easily set off like a grenade?"

They laughed and quietly puffed on their cigars.

"She thinks a lot of you, John."

"I think she's just used to me being around. She tolerates me."

Max chuckled. "Consider this, son. Roman must have known something serious was in her heart or he wouldn't have come up with that crazy will. And I know damn well he knew you were giving her the big eye. You have no one but yourself to blame for your present situation." He laughed aloud and leaned his head back against the chair.

A long comfortable silence laid over them until John groaned softly. "I'm not complaining."

* * * *

Bella glanced forlornly at the telephone on the nightstand. She had stationed herself in the middle of John's bed and typed the report for her employer, sending it with a grimace of finality.

She wanted John to call her, but what would she say to him? It was obvious he was not going to stop talking down to her in his macho, condescending, smart-ass way. He gave her no credit for any intelligence. She was pissed off.

Pulling his pillow to her face, she sniffed and hugged it to her breast. Remembering their difficult moment of uncertainty, she threw the pillow on the floor. He didn't remember the passion and her absolute surrender of just a few hours ago. She wouldn't be so easy the next time.

Pushing the computer aside, she listened to the whine of the vacuum cleaner coming from somewhere in the house. She had forgotten about Ellie until now. She got up from the bed and slipped on the fuzzy house shoes John had obligingly brought to her once.

Boredom made her eager for companionship and Bella laughed at herself for being a baby with her constant need for human contact. Attending three and four parties a week had been her way of beating the frightening aspect of being alone.

Bella peered around the door of the den and smiled at Ellie when she looked up from her work. She waited until the vacuum was quiet before going into the walnut paneled room. "I didn't mean to bother you."

Ellie set the sweeper aside and inhaled several times, laughing as she pressed her palms to her lower back. "Heck, you're not bothering me." She motioned for Bella to follow her into the kitchen. "Let's have a cup of coffee. Time for a break anyway."

"That sounds good." Bella nodded and trailed after the cheerful woman.

"Great. I made a coffee cake, too."

The beautiful baked goods displayed on the counter amazed Bella. She took a slice of the coffee cake and nibbled the edge. Her eyes rounded and she took a hefty bite and chewed with pleasure. "You made this?"

"Why, sure. Probably not as good as yours though."

"I can't cook." There was neither stammer nor shame in her admission. Bella had never had a reason to know how to whip up nourishing meals, until now. She laid her cake down. "Will you teach me how to cook? I just need to know for five months."

Ellie took a long drink of coffee and eyed Bella over the rim of her cup. She set her coffee down and smiled. "That's okay. Never was a need for you to be sweating over a cook stove before now." She wiped her hands on a napkin before easing into the cooking lessons idea. "It's not hard, Bella. I'll work you up some really quick menus of things any man will like. They don't really care about what they're eating, just how it tastes." She laughed and poured Bella a second cup of coffee.

Excitement touched Bella and she gestured toward the three-layer coconut cake on its crystal stand. "I want to make that and standing rib roast and a rack of lamb and shrimp cocktails."

She stood and picked a shred of coconut from the cake stand, popping it into her mouth. Ellie shook her head and touched Bella's arm. "I don't know about all that. Let’s keep it simple. Men like uncomplicated food." She arched her brows. "Well, that goes for everything else."

"You’re probably right, Ellie. I'd just like to do something to make John happy."

"I think you need something to do. The women around here are having a county garage sale tomorrow. Want to join in?"

"I don't know. Do I have to cook?"

Ellie laughed and shook her head. "No. All you do is gather up anything you were fixing to throw out or don't want anymore and try to sell it. There ain't nothin that can't be sold. Make you some spending money." Ellie worked her brows up and down to emphasize her meaning.

Whatever she meant, Bella was eager to join the party. "Okay. I'll do it. There's still time for me to clean out the closets in my apartment."

"We start early. These sale people are up with the chickens."

Bella wasn't positive how early that would be, but didn't ask. She figured her questions just made her sound more ignorant all the time. Wonderful. She had something to do until her next assignment. Plus, she found out Ellie wasn't so bad, unless it was all a show and she was really setting a trap for her. Whichever, it didn't matter.

As she drove off toward Dallas, she had to force herself not to make a surprise visit to John's office. That would be the last thing he would want her to do. *Sure, before you were Mrs. Lawless, it would have been a thrill to charge into his office and aggravate him. No more.*

Pleasing him was uppermost on her mind.

Feeling better than she had all day, Bella sighed when her apartment complex came into view. She experienced no sense of belonging or comfort as she once had. That emotion was reserved for John these days.

Once she was inside her pricey apartment, Bella hurried around the bedroom, gathering up armloads of clothing, shoes and handbags. The one item put safely aside was her cherished wedding ensemble.

She touched the protective plastic cover that draped over the sheer white and silver fabric and sighed. She loved the fact John remembered what she had worn that night. Warmth streamed through her as the idea he might care for her gained momentum. But, wait. He was, after all, a typical horny male and only remembered how much the outfit revealed.

She hung the delicate garment up and pushed it to the back of the closet, going on with her work. After several hours, Bella had gathered enough items to fill her sports car to overflowing.

The spotless kitchen was her final room to search and she picked up a few things she figured would make life better at the ranch. Her European waffle iron and Fostoria ice tea glasses would bring a small touch of home to their table. The rest she could come back for. After rummaging around in the silverware drawers, she was ready to leave the apartment. From now on, he would have only wonderful things to remember about her.

A stop at her favorite jewelry designer's shop proved to be worthwhile. Happiness wrapped around Bella while she inspected the ring she had chosen for John. The wide gold band with its large onyx setting looked honest and strong, like him. It would have to be altered up several sizes, and though the idea wasn't pleasing to her, she would have to wait. In five days, she would be able to give it to her husband.

The trip back to the ranch was delayed while Bella shopped in a food mart. Her eyes went to things she knew and she quickly filled her cart and checked out. The desire to turn the volume up on her CD player was hard to resist, but she did. John kept the music low and she liked it that way, too. For now.

When she drove around the curved driveway in front of the house, she could see Ellie carrying things to the double garage. Excitement gripped her. This would be her first garage sale. She found a choice spot in the shade and parked, getting out and waving to Ellie.

"I found a lot of things. Is it okay?"

Ellie eyed the contents of the car. "You should make more than a little spending cash for that haul."

Bella wanted to show the obviously wiser woman she could get things done and dove into the job of carrying her things into the garage. "I'll take one side and you take the other. Maybe I should move some of that old junk outside. We'll have more room."

Ellie followed her and pointed out a large steel rack. "Plenty of room on this." She tested the material of a light wool suit that Bella had tossed over it. "You decide on prices for your things?"

She had to ask strangers for money? Bella's eyes widened in shock. "Oh, I think as cheap as possible."

"That’s smart. Things will sell a lot faster priced right. You'll clean up."

Clean up? "I just want enough money to buy a gift for John." Bella went back to pulling things out of the car.

Ellie laughed and pulled some small stringed tags from her pocket. "I'll price and you sort."

"Okay. But I think I'll move that junk out to the side of the garage." Bella pointed to what appeared to be a canoe and something on wheels under a dusty cover.

Ellie kept on writing on the tags and nodded. "I'll help. Men don't have light weight junk."

Bella stood beside whatever it was covered with an olive drab tarp and sighed. "What would anyone want with something this color?"

She pulled the tarp aside for Ellie to look at the chrome wheels of a black and red motorcycle. They both shrugged. Bella steered and Ellie balanced the back end until the bike was outside and propped against the garage. They high-fived and went back to work.

The afternoon flew by as Bella worked furiously, hanging the small price tags and arranging her table displays. She paused to wipe sweat from her face when Ellie carried in a pitcher of iced tea.

"That looks wonderful." Taking a long drink from her glass, Bella looked around with a smile of satisfaction. "I'll fix dinner for John tonight so you won't have to bother."

Ellie arched her brows and smiled. "I gotcha. You won't see me again until breakfast time."

Bella abandoned the garage for the kitchen after the sun started getting low in the west. She had so much to do before John got home. She stood in the middle of the room for a time, wondering where to start. Relief washed over her when she remembered the bags of groceries she had brought from town.

But first, she had to make herself irresistible in his eyes. That called for a bubble bath and lots of perfumes and oils. Shivers of delight stroked her body while she bathed and prepared for her lover. She washed her hair in a favorite cherry bark and almond shampoo and rinsed it in water laced with her perfume.

As she got out of the tub, she noticed the time. Oh Lord, it was so late and she was so far behind. No time to rinse the tub or dry her long hair. An ankle length sari gown of pale green was what her hand touched first in the closet and she grabbed it, pulling the dress on as she ran for the kitchen.

The floor felt cool under her bare feet as she opened boxes of crackers and cans. After rinsing salad greens, she took half a dozen packages of deli meats from the refrigerator, laying out the slices on a plate. The assortment of cheeses added some class to the plain looking display and a center dish of pickles and olives completed her creation.

A hissing sound caught her attention and she moaned in despair to see her pot of chicken noodle soup boiling over. She frantically tore half a roll of paper towels from the dispenser and wiped at the spill, near tears when she heard John's Jeep pull into the driveway.

She was already embarrassed by the smell of scorched soup, and now the ice cream she'd forgotten to put in the freezer was running through the bottom of the grocery bag. Her frantic turn to grab a tea towel sent her flying across the floor and onto her butt. She had skidded in a huge pool of melted ice cream.

John came into the kitchen looking down at her before she could recover and present a more mature appearance.

"Hello, honey." He lifted her up to hug her close. "Whatever you're cooking sure smells good."

Her smile was tremulous but she bestowed her adoration on him with no reservation. "I hope you like it, John. It's our one month anniversary dinner."

Chapter Twelve

John wanted to laugh. He needed to laugh. His gut hurt from holding it back. Instead, he held Bella close and struggled to pull himself together.

"Our anniversary?" He looked over her head at the complete mess the kitchen was in. "And you're cooking for me, too?"

Her arms hugged his waist harder. "Yes, but I'm afraid it isn't quite like I planned." She swiped at her skirt.

He drew her up on her toes to kiss her, nibbling her lips gently. "That's okay. You taste good, Bella. That's enough for me."

She leaned back to meet his gaze, her smile soft and a little crooked. "Wait until you see what I have for dessert."

Her sweet words made him glad he had come straight home from work. No drinks with his buddies or ball game could compare to this. He offered her a hand.

"Want me to swab the deck in here while you de-ice cream your cute little feet?" Quickly amending his suggestion, he gestured toward the stove. "I'm hungry as a bear, so don't be long, okay?"

"Okay. But don't taste anything until I get back." She gingerly stepped over the mess on the floor.

He chuckled and nodded, waiting until she was out of the room before attacking the mess. He took his jacket off and hung it over a chair, then dragged out the mop and pail from the utility closet.

When the floor was spotless, he wiped the counters and cleaned the stovetop off. He couldn't resist looking in the pot that bubbled merrily along with its cargo of canned soup. *Easy, boy. You have to eat it and like it.*

He grinned when he found the packaged cookies and cannoli. Bella had a sweet tooth. He should have thought to bring her a box of candy, or at the very least, a huge bouquet of daisies.

He looked out the back door and then stepped out on the patio, glanced over his shoulder and headed for the rail fence to snap half a dozen roses off the tangled vines. His heart pounded like crazy by the time he got back in the house and had stuck the flowers in a glass filled with water. He jumped when he heard her footsteps.

"You didn't taste anything, did you?" Bella stopped still, and looked at the homespun bouquet on the table. "John, it’s the most beautiful thing I have ever seen."

He couldn't speak. Bella looked like she was washed in pink moonlight. The gown she had put on hugged her soft curves like delicate slick strokes of seduction. He had no idea what kind of material the low-cut dress was made of and he didn't care. He just wanted to touch it. Her lovely little breasts spilled over the neckline, tempting him with all their pink and pale gold lushness.

Hell and damnation, she still didn't know how hot he was for her. How was he supposed to eat and keep his hands to himself until she gave him a cue to move in?

"Baby, compared to you, they look like weeds." He leaned against the counter and smiled at her. "Is there anything else I can do for you, Flower?"

It didn't happen often, but Bella seemed unsure of herself. She clasped her hands in front of her and bit her lip. Her complexion glowed with an undertone of rose. Bella was exquisite. How the hell had she been single until he came along?

John took the initiative and gallantly pulled a chair out for her. "Sit my lovely, and I'll serve you."

"But John, I should be serving you. It's our anniversary."

He stomped down his vile excess testosterone and nodded in agreement. "I think we can do this together." He arched his brow and smiled at her, certain he must look like a big bad wolf to her.

She went into action then, getting soup bowls and spoons. He grabbed a sleeve of crackers and dumped them in a bread basket. From the corner of his eye, he watched her move the dishes around until they were exactly aligned across from one another. He grinned as she plopped a huge bunch of grapes on a plate and placed a piece of silverware beside them.

"Okay, ma'am. I'm serving your soup now. Please sit."

She smiled and took her chair, licking her lips while he ladled soup into her bowl.

Damn if it didn't look good since she was there with him. When he sat down across from her, he looked up to see her gazing at him in a way that cradled his heart. She had looked at him with desire, hate and irritation, but this was tenderness.

"Happy Anniversary, John."

"Happy Anniversary, Bella."

They lifted their juice glasses and toasted with the Kool-Aid she had made earlier.

He took his first bite of the scorched soup and smacked his lips. "My compliments to the cook."

After her first bite, she laid her spoon down and ate crackers and luncheon meat. "I'm glad you like it, John." After a moment, she giggled. "You don't have to eat it. It's horrible."

"No, really." He held his hands up to stop her. "You've outdone yourself."

She smiled and ducked her chin. "I think I need to do something to make up for the gross dinner." She picked up the small instrument from the tray of grapes and waved it around. "I'll peel you a grape if you desire."

John grinned and moved his bowl to the side, watching her with total fascination. She was probably the only woman that brought grape shears to a supper of canned soup and deli meat. What the hell. Nothing mattered except the smile she laid on him right now.

"That would be real nice." He knew that had sounded supremely stupid and tried to recover. He felt redemption was near. His jacket was draped over the back of his chair, making it easy for him to dip in his pocket and bring out the ring box.

"John, I'll bring it to you." She smiled seductively, moistening her lips.

"No, babe. I'll come to you." He stood and went to stand behind her chair, working the box open and letting the ring roll into his palm. A throb of excitement raced over his body as he leaned over her shoulder and dropped the ring into her cleavage.

She laughed and shivered a little, touching her breast. "What was that? It's cold."

"Sorry, Flower." His breath caught while she fished between her breasts and finally drew the ring out. He was on edge. It took her an awful long time to look at the ring. She held it in her palm and her hand shook.

She spoke in a whisper. "John, it's so beautiful." There were tears in her eyes. "You didn't forget."

"Forget something so important? How could I?"

She stood and held the ring out to him. "Put it on my finger, please."

The tremble in his hand was worse than the first time they did this ring thing. He took the ring and slid it onto her finger and met her teary gaze with a crooked grin. "Looks perfect to me."

Her breath was shaky and soft as she pressed her hand to his heart and admired her wedding ring. "I never dreamed you would remember."

He covered her hand with his and kissed her forehead. "I remember everything about you, Bella."

He loved her way of pressing into him and soft-soaping her way into his heart. "Do you remember last night?" She had no idea how far she'd sent him into space with their lovemaking.

"Yes, I do." He groaned softly, putting his arm around her waist. "Do you want to refresh my memory?"

"Yes, I do, and this time I want a lot more."

The urge to take her on the spot was stronger than his self-control. Catching her close, he picked her up in his arms. "Lady, your dessert will be served in my bed."

* * * *

Bella clung to John's strong body while he came, clutching his tight rear in her hands while the out-of-body sensation eased away, leaving her drenched and weak. The very thought that she was really in his bed, in his arms, ignited her libido and she moved against him until a flash of sweet fire blazed in her core a final time.

"Dessert was wonderful, John." She stretched under his warm weight and eased her arms above her head to sprawl in perfect bliss.

"You're an unbelievable woman." John caught her lip between his teeth, and then sucked until she sighed in surrender. He played with her hair for a moment then kissed her gently. "Come on, let's take a shower." He stood and dropped his condom in the wastebasket. "I left a few of these in the shower stall."

"Enticement will take you far." She laughed and lifted her arms to let him pull her up to stand in front of him. Her eyes devoured him as he led her into the bathroom.

"So, pretty face." He leaned over to remove a cellophane wrapper from his heel. "It's SeaWorld fantasy time."

Bella's breath quickened just watching him lean in the shower stall to get the rain shower started. She was so in love with his lean muscular body and never tired of inspecting his generous sex. Her palms tingled in want of touching his chest and shoulders, his flat belly and strong back. But, most of all, she loved being in his arms and hearing him call her his sex goddess.

He stepped under the lovely fall of warm water and made room for her. He had been right, there were several condoms in the toiletry rack. She pointed to his stash and smacked his rear.

"Remind me to show you which appendage those go on."

He knelt and pulled her hips against his face, darting his tongue in and out of her navel, kissing and tasting the softness of her folds. She had wanted this for so long, dreamed of it and now while it happened, it was too intense and joyous to explain.

She experienced a pleasure and a pain that was new and she feared it would elude her if she reached for it again. She gripped his ears as he tasted her delicate inner folds, letting him hold her still until her knees buckled and she draped over his shoulder. His voice sounded far away when he spoke.

"I love the way you come, baby."

"Not half as much as I do," she said softly. Her hand went to his member as he stood and drew her against him. She reached around him and took one of the packages from the shelf, breaking the cellophane.

"I'm hot, baby." He rocked against her.

"That's the idea." She gripped him and moved her fingers up and down his hard length, reaching down to cup his scrotum in a firm hold.

"I see, you're not going to let me be nice and wait until we're having sex, are you?"

"No." She wanted him to do just that, and smiled in a bewitching tease at the prospect of making him reach orgasm with her simply touching him. "Go ahead."

"No, I want us to come together. Now."

She laughed and popped the condom out of its package and worked it onto his engorged member. "Fine with me." She gasped as he lifted her up and entered her in a measured hard thrust. "Umm, cowboy."

He didn't treat her with kid gloves this time, pulling her legs up to his waist and pushing her against the shower wall. She heard the splash of water and tasted his mouth with his every thrust and the moving tease of his tongue. He stole her very last inhibition, her will to say no to anything and her desire to be just one person alone any more.

He took her high above ordinary sex into his rough-and-tumble, go-for-broke lovemaking and his heart melting kisses.

The dull squeak of her back sliding against the tiled wall roused Bella from a deep euphoria. A new blaze burst up from her cleft where his thrusting hips sent her chasing a new uplifting need. She bit his shoulder in her quest for release, laughing when he moaned.

"Did you like that?" she asked, spanking his rear.

"I'll tell you in a minute, you little cat."

He held her still, kissing her so deeply her heart threatened to stop and her legs went weak as cotton candy, kissing her until she became part of the fire of climax, coming with him and slipped into a near faint.

"You've got to stop doing that, Bella."

"What?" she asked, puzzled by the look of concern on his face.

He stared at her with a crooked grin. "Going out like that. Where'd you go?"

"I've been saving it up for so long, I can't help it."

"Thank you, baby. That's the sexiest thing anyone has ever said to me."

She didn't want to hear what other women had said to him. Right now she was so into the way he let her down, the slide of their bodies gliding slick and warm against each other. The soaping playtime was pure joy of being caressed by his big, long-fingered hands and brought to mind-numbing climax again while he held her in a hard embrace.

"My God, John. I'll melt away if you keep doing that."

"Want me to stop?" He cupped her breasts and squeezed, smiling into her eyes.

"Don't even think about it." She pressed her mouth to his and slid her tongue into his, caressing the warm underside of his lips until he shut the water off and carried her to their bed.

* * * *

Bella had to agree with Ellie that it was a perfect day for a garage sale. Sunny skies and a gentle breeze seemed to be an incentive for people to be out. A steady stream of shoppers drifted in and out of the garage all day. Bella couldn't believe the amount of cash collecting in her cigar box cash register.

Ellie seemed to know a great deal about selling used things, her smile working wonders on the male shoppers. Bella tried to be a sales person but felt intimidated when people asked how much less she would take for items. That was when she called for help from Ellie.

Glad to sit back and observe a pro, Bella poured herself a glass of ice-cold lemonade and took a sip. Before she could set the glass down, someone tapped her shoulder, startling her. Her hand shook, and she turned to face a bear of a man dressed in leather and denim.

They stared at each other for a few seconds, and then he shifted his considerable weight from one side to the other. He gestured over his shoulder with his thumb. "Ma'am. How much you asking for the bike?"

Her gaze strayed to the big silver buckle on his belt while she thought over his question. "I'm sorry, bicycle? I don't think we have one."

He grinned at her. "Yeah, the one outside."

Bella considered consulting with Ellie, but didn't. She followed the huge man out to the spot where she had summarily dispatched the junk. "Oh, that one."

She was amazed by his grinning reaction to the silly looking motorbike. She quietly observed his gentle caress to the black leather seat and loving touch to the chrome handlebars and fancy detailed gas tank with its Indian in full head dress. He almost crooned while his fingers traveled over the gleaming spoke wheels.

"What're you asking for her?"

"For her?" Bella looked frantically for Ellie.

"How much you want for this bike?"

"Oh." Bella's untried salesmanship kicked in. "What are you offering?"

He scratched his jaw and scuffed his boot on the grass. "Well, the shape the Indian's in, I'd go as high as five hundred."

The amount wasn't a great deal to her, but for a useless item like he wanted, it was phenomenal. "Sold."

Before she could blink, he was counting out the bills in her hand and grinning like a Cheshire cat.

"She's a beauty, ma'am. I'll be loading her up now."

Bella was consumed with the glow of success while the man threw the ugly tarp aside and pushed his purchase to his truck parked in the driveway. With the help of a waiting friend, the bike was loaded into the back of the truck and he drove away.

"Ellie." With her heart pounding in delight, Bella shared the news of her good fortune. "Look. You'll never guess how much that junky old bike was worth."

Ellie stopped folding the sweater in her hands and laughed. "Good job. I made a few extra dollars by tossing in some fishing gear Buck had thrown on the trash heap. Amazing what people will buy."

Bella stuffed her share of the money in her cash drawer. "When we are finished here, I'm going in to Dallas."

Ellie grinned at her. "Buying more clothes?"

"Oh, no. To get John's wedding ring if it's ready. He doesn't have one yet."

"You're kidding. Better get that ring on him quick. Too many gals think a man with no ring is a man with no woman."

Bella nodded and bit her lip. How many times had she made ugly comments about Ellie? Now, here she was, getting marital advice from her. It seemed she had been terribly wrong about a lot of things.

"Thanks Ellie. Hopefully, by tonight, he'll be branded."

* * * *

John parked under the gnarled old apple tree near the garage, thinking the ladies might need to get back in the building. He grinned when he noticed the silver-gray town car sitting near the front entrance of the house. His parents had come calling.

Roscoe made a beeline for him and wagged his tail furiously for attention, whining a little for sympathy. "Okay, boy. Did the ladies ignore you today?" John laughed and leaned over to pick up the blue tarp that had been covering the Indian.

He walked around into the garage, intending to cover the bike but found nothing but an empty space where it had been stored. The garage was strewn with hat boxes, clothing and shoes. No Indian. Apprehension gripped his gut. No, she couldn't have done that. She couldn't have sold the bike.

Wadding up the tarp, he threw it against the wall, and stalked to the back door of the house. The screen door made its usual gruesome sound and alerted Bella that he was home.

She came into the kitchen, her eyes glowing. "Hello, darling." She winced when he avoided her embrace.

John held his breath as he looked at her. "Bella, the bike. Where is it?"

She looked at him as if he were nuts. "I don't know."

His voice rose in volume. "Don't know? Sure you do. What did you do with it?"

Her brows went up and her smile brightened. "Oh, that. I sold it for five hundred dollars. The man said it was a real bargain even if the bike did need a paint job."

God damn it! She was looking at him like he should be telling her what a good thing she had done. She may as well have sold his first born son.

"Bella." He grabbed her arm and drew her close. "Listen to me. Where did he go?"

She drew back and scowled at him. "Stop it. I don't know where he went. He wore gang clothing is all I remember."

John's stomach turned over and knotted tightly. "Why did you take it upon yourself to do that? You don't need money, God damn it!"

He didn't care about the tears misting in her eyes as she spoke. "I wanted to pay for your ring with money I had earned, John."

"Aw, Jesus." He couldn't hide the raw anger and frustration consuming him "Did it ever occur to you that I might want to keep it, that the fucking bike meant something to me?" He couldn't believe she backed away from him as if he might hit her. That only served to make him angrier. "Bella, you're selfish and don't give a damn about anyone, never considering anyone but yourself." He held his arms out from his sides in utter frustration. "What are you? Twelve?"

He felt the strangling sensation of wanting to use every cuss word he knew but swallowed them down. He noticed his parents looking in the direction of the noise from the sunroom door. Bella sniffed and lifted her chin.

"Your parents are here, and we were planning to have dinner in town before they drive back to Austin."

He took Bella's hand and led her outside. "That doesn't seem likely now, does it?"

"John, what can I do to make up for it? I didn't mean to hurt you."

"Do?" He couldn't believe she was so clueless, never aware of the real world. "Nothing. "

John barely heard his father calling his name.

"John. What's going on out here?" His father gave him the hottest glare he had ever gotten. "Your mother is concerned."

Bella tried to pull away, but John wouldn't let her escape what she had caused. Not this time, not like he had always done in the past.

Chapter Thirteen

Bella wanted to die on the spot, to slink into a dark cave to be alone with her anguish. John held her fast by his side, almost as if he wanted her to face as much embarrassment as he could heap on her. He met his father's stern gaze without flinching.

She had been called names and undergone harsh, angry, jealous criticism. She had been called ugly, vulgar, dirty names, but the things John had said tore her heart out. She finally yanked her arm from his grasp.

"I'm sorry we've been so long out here, Hall." She swallowed with difficulty and wet her dry lips. "John wanted to show me something." She wiped her cheeks with her palms. "We'll be right in."

"Stop it, Bella. Dad heard. He knows what you're like."

Hall stood with his hands in his pockets and solemnly gazed at John. "For the first time in my life, I'm ashamed of my son."

"Sorry, sir. I feel I am within the boundaries of reason to be pissed off under the circumstances."

John's mother approached them slowly, appearing nervous and close to tears. Bella clasped her hands together to hide their trembling and tried to sound cheerful. "Mary, it's all just a simple mistake. Shall we go have our coffee?"

Mary's cheeks were pale and her eyes touched Bella with concern. "I think it would be best if we left now. In-laws are in the way at a time like this."

Bella couldn't stand up under the pitying smiles and John's dark glare. She ran inside the house, stopping in the kitchen to grab a bottle from the wine rack. She could hear them out on the patio, John's father giving his horrible son a chewing out and his mother adding her two cents worth.

She heard Hall's admonishment first. "John, you cannot speak to your wife in that lowdown manner."

Then John's come back. "Dad, please butt out. Bella sold something of mine that meant a lot to me. She's reckless and doesn't give a damn about anyone but herself. I've had it with her."

A softer voice broke into the baritones as Mary spoke up. "You have hurt her terribly, John. It is imperative you apologize to her immediately. Your marriage will not survive moments like this if you don't ask forgiveness."

"Mom, I love you, but I know Bella better than you do. "

Then their voices became muffled, too faint for Bella to understand. They obviously had moved away from the house. Bella didn't want to be the cause of a family disagreement. She was a member in name only and shouldn't be listening. She worked the cork out of the bottle and hurried down the hall and exited the house through John's bedroom door.

The feeling of being trapped wasn't new to her, but there was no way she could survive with so much pain to bear. She needed a place to hide and grieve.

Out in the yard with the innocent roses and leftover garage sale sign, she looked around for a friendly place to unburden her heart. Dark clouds gathered overhead and she paid little attention to the ominous sky. A gust of wind charged across the backyard, picking up the green tarp that had covered the cause of her heartache.

"Hell with it," she mumbled, and took a hefty drink of her wine. It warmed her to the core and she took another drink. She hadn't eaten enough dinner and the sweet wine raced to her head.

Lightning tore through the dark clouds and slammed into the horizon miles away. For the first time, a coming storm didn't scare Bella. She was only concerned with getting away from the ugly scene that had ended a beautiful dream.

A whirring, grinding sound made her look up. The windmill. The blades spun so fast they were a silver blur. Didn't matter. The wine was tasting better and she sobbed freely with no one to hear or see her. Clutching the bottle, she easily scaled the narrow ladder to the top and climbed onto the small platform.

She wasn't scared of the huge pinwheel that screamed in the wind. Everything was going just swell. She tipped the bottle up and cried harder.

Wiping her eyes, she peered down at the house and stables, and then stoically watched as John's parents drove away. There was John, looking up at the sky before he hurried into the house.

She sobbed then, ashamed of being in love with a man who wished she would disappear.

After taking another long drink, Bella sat down and dangled her feet off the platform and swiped at the tears on her cheeks. She hiccupped and giggled. "The sheep look like cotton balls," she observed aloud, then laughed and took another drink.

A rowdy commotion coming from below her perch made Bella look down. Ellie's border collie, Roscoe, ran circles around the windmill tower and kept an eye on her all the while.

She waved her hand at the dog. "Roscoe. Go home. You'll get in trouble for making a fuss."

After forcing the last of the wine down, Bella fell back to stare up at the black clouds.

She cried aloud and mournfully. The cold rain that fell on her face didn't stop the tears. Before she closed her eyes, she saw lightning pitchfork overhead and heard thunder rumble, but she didn't flinch. She was too unhappy to fear anything now.

Someone called to her. The voice was familiar and far away. It came again, stronger this time. John was yelling at her for some reason. She leaned over to yell back at him.

"No need to bother yourself anymore, John. I'm moving up here."

He didn't seem to hear her. "Hell with you." She took off one shoe and hurled it down to get his attention.

Her grin was crooked as she observed John and the playful Roscoe fighting over the shoe. The dog won and ran toward Buck and Ellie's house. "Heavy, heavy over thy head," she mumbled and dropped the other shoe.

At last he looked up and zeroed in on her hiding place. He gestured emphatically, arms spread and palms up. "Bella, get the hell down here." He pointed toward the southwest.

"There's a cyclone wind coming this way."

She waved in a dismissive way. "Storm? Storm you say, Mr. Pilot man," she chortled. "Let it."

He gripped the ladder, shouting up at her and over the wind. "Come down, now. It's not safe up there."

His demand for her to think of her safety seemed to torch her well-hidden fear and personal pain. She screamed out in her despair.

"What do I care? I don't want to be safe." She stared in shock after the bottle that fell from her grasp and hit the ladder on its way to the ground. "Oops." She laughed and waved down to John.

He was obviously angry, shouting at her again. "Bella."

"John." Her heavy hair clasp was next to dive to the earth.

"Ouch. Now, damn it, Bella."

She peered down at him, the tall man with the thick dark hair and wonderful, green eyes. John—the bastard that couldn't love her.

"I tried to hurt you, you horse's ass. Get back to the house where it's safe and secure and you don't need anyone."

He had a foot on the first rung. "I know you're pissed off, Bella. I don't give a damn about that. Just haul your carcass down here right now."

A flash of white-hot lightning lit up the roiling clouds and brought a deafening crash of thunder as company. The powerful display sizzled above Bella's head and she held her arms up, yearning to climb to its center.

Standing at the edge of the platform, she sobbed and emptied her soul of its pain and dark terror of being alone. Her long hair tossed in the wind and whipped her as if in agreement that she deserved punishment.

"Bella, are you tanked? Can you cause any more trouble tonight?" He rubbed his forehead and looked down as if saying a prayer.

"Didn't you hear what I said?" To make her point clear, she tore her T-shirt off and tossed it off the ledge. "I'm supposed to be dead."

"That's nuts, Bella." He stood back and waved his hands in desperation. "You'll be all right. I'll think of something."

"You don't understand. I always went on their trips, but not the last one." She swiped at her hair and sobbed. "I was supposed to die with them, can't you see that? I should have been with my mother."

John held his arms up to her. "Of course you're alive, and I want you to stay that way. Now get back from the ledge and sit down."

"Kiss my ass, John. Why should I? I wanted you to love me, wanted to love you. But no, you didn't want that. You're a cold and miserable bastard, John."

She worked her skirt off and threw it over the ledge.

"Damn it, Bella. I know you're foxed, but you know better. Sit down."

"Sure. You're just worried that someone will see me being nasty." Her laugh caught and was carried off in the wind. Her hand was on the waist of her panties. "Your job as my warden was over months ago. Time for you to find someone who needs you. I sure the hell don't."

He stood looking around and up at her as if he was hoping for a miracle, wiping rain from his face. "If you don't come down, I'll have to get Buck to drag you home."

"Buck?" She was incredulous at the suggestion. "Coward. What's the matter with you? Come and get me. Chicken pants. Yellow bird."

She sank to her knees and wept, hating him, hating herself. To make matters worse, he was coming up the ladder, looking too big and too heavy for the spindly contraption.

Unable to help herself, she kept her gaze riveted on him while he worked his way up to where she sat, and then crawled to the back edge to wait when he topped the ladder and glared in her direction. He glanced over her head and looked down, groaning as he crawled onto the platform. He gripped her arm, then promptly pitched forward, face down in a dead faint.

Bella stared wide-eyed at the big man lying in a crumpled heap and screamed in helpless outrage at her life. "John." She poked his arm. "Get up. I don't want you up here."

Would she ever be able to stop lying about her feelings for him? Not want him with her? In truth she was so glad he was there, even passed out or whatever was wrong with him. He was big and comforting and the rain was coming harder now, and hail smacked her with punishing little bites.

Why was she so stupid, taking her clothes off and letting him see how vulnerable she was? He didn't care how much she ached for her Mommy and Daddy. Most of all, he didn't care that she ached for him.

With a hard sob and deep show of devotion, Bella lay down with John and covered his body with her own, shielding his head with her hands and locking her legs with his to keep them from being swept off the platform in the high winds. A high-pitched scream startled her and she slowly realized it had been her scream when a piece of sheet metal clanged into the blades of the windmill. The terrifying noises made her cling more protectively to John while she murmured in his ear to not be afraid.

She had no idea of how long they had been up on the frightening platform, but the storm finally abated and moved away. Bella sat up and grimaced, trying to straighten her cramped legs. John groaned in his discomfort. He turned onto his back and gazed into her eyes.

* * * *

"Bella, I swear you'll be the death of me." He pulled her down where she huddled on his chest.

"John." She hugged his waist and studied his face for a minute. "What happened to you? I thought you were dead."

He grinned weakly. "Sorry about that. It's the first time my vertigo completely kicked my ass." He tried to sit up. She leaned against him.

"Vertigo?" She smacked his arm. "I hate you for coming up here. You're insane. I didn't ask you to save me."

He was slowly recovering and her smart mouth fired his desire to vent his anger.

He grabbed her wrist and scowled. "Me, insane? What about you? We're back to seventeen again." He inhaled roughly and sat up, pushing her off his legs. "So, we're both crazy. Let's get the hell off this damn thing."

She was wearing nothing but her skivvies. He started unbuttoning his shirt, planning to give it to her. She noticed what he was doing and mocked him.

"Your deep concern touches me to the quick. Such sacrifices you have made on my behalf. Keep your shirt."

She sounded wounded, but he was too angry to care. "Go to the jungles of Peru. I sure as hell didn't want to come up here for your spoiled ass." He shoved her hand away when she tried to touch him. "It's probably funny to you, but because of this little dizzy spell thing I have, my career went to hell. I can't fly, I can't climb." He got to his feet and looked at her.

He saw new emotions in the expression that played over her gorgeous face. Surprise? Sympathy? She opened her mouth to speak several times before the words tumbled from her lips.

"I didn't know that. You never bothered telling me the reason you left the Navy."

"Why I left wouldn't have been important to you."

They stared at one another for a time, until a fresh rain shower reminded them of the perilous perch they were on.

"Well, I hate you for putting yourself in danger. I didn't want you to get hurt, John, and I didn't think it was funny."

"Whatever you think, Bella Fleur, I'm still a man, a man that's supposed to protect you. You make it awful hard to do that."

Like a svelte cat, Bella stood and looked down at the cluttered ground below. "You're free from all responsibility as of this moment, John."

He got to his feet to stand behind her. "Whatever the hell you say, lady." He put his hand on her shoulder. "Just crawl down off this thing and I'll leave you alone."

"Promise?" She jerked away from his touch. "And don't blame me for your problems. I am giving you the door, Mr. Superman."

What a bitch. Here he was risking his lousy neck for her and she was calling him a coward. Well, maybe she was right, but he was sick of her treating him like a cabana boy. His words dripped sarcasm. "You're really something, Flower. Fifty feet in the air with nothing on but your hide and still saucy as hell. Wow. No wonder I'm so damn happy and content."

"Kiss my ass, John."

Before he could react to her quip, Bella was already on the ladder and moving down it at a dizzying speed.

He couldn't think of anything but getting back on solid earth, he would be grateful just to feel the dirt under his feet again. Humiliation stuck to him like a dirty shirt as he closed his eyes and slid down to plant his feet on the ladder rungs, one at a time. It had seemed so much easier climbing up.

He could breathe normally again when his feet touched the wet grass. John was grateful she was safe, but that didn't keep him from wanting to wring her neck. When he managed to stand on his own, he snarled at her.

"If this is your last act of idiocy for the night, I'm going to bed." He was desperate to get to his room to lie down, but he had to hit the bathroom first. His gut was turning upside down and his head was spinning crazily.

"Fine." She ran after him, tugging on his shirtsleeve. "Want me to wake you if I think of some other way to scare the hell out of you?"

"You've done it all, lady. There's nothing left."

She held her tongue for a second, apparently thinking over his words. "That sounded like a challenge, and you'll see I've only just begun."

Chapter Fourteen

Bella hadn't slept well since their ordeal on the windmill. John avoided her, going out of his way to be gone when she woke up and coming home hours after she had gone to bed. He didn't know she couldn't close her eyes until the rumble of his Jeep in the driveway assured her he was home.

The ugly thought that he might be consorting with other women ate at her confidence, but she fought it away. What did it matter? John didn't love her.

After hearing him come in the house on the third night of not seeing him, she decided she couldn't go on with the standoff. Bella got out of bed and went to the door separating their rooms and boldly opened it.

"John."

"You're in the wrong room."

"I'm only visiting."

"How charitable. What the hell do you want?"

"It's not charity I bring." She moved toward his bed and flipped on the overhead light. "One of us has to be adult about this."

He sat up and glared at her. "Did you bring a stand in for yourself?"

"You didn't mean that." She wanted to sound breezy but his greeting had hurt. "I want to sleep with you. I don't like sleeping without you." While she gazed down at him, she longed to jump on top of him and kiss those angry looking lips. "I came in to tell you that all this avoiding me isn't necessary. I won't speak to you unless you ask me a question. And, if you want, I'll move back to my apartment in Dallas. I'll do whatever it takes to make up for what I did to you."

He sat up and rubbed his eyes, then groaned. "Bella, you can't imagine how much I longed to hear those words for four long, miserable years." He leaned back against his pillows and gazed at her. "Too little and too damn late. Now, close the door on your way out."

Bella chose to ignore his order to leave. Instead, she mulled over the part where he'd said he had waited for her to treat him right. How pathetic. She couldn't recall a time he had been chivalrous or just plain friendly. And she couldn't remember being too generous with him. They just plain rubbed each other the wrong way from the first breath they shared.

The day she had tried to wipe from her mind was looming in the future. Their divorce would sever all ties and she would not survive without John. She wanted something of him to cherish forever and she wondered why she hadn't thought of it sooner.

Leaning over to pick up a nightgown she had worn to his bed, Bella sighed and held it to her nose. His aftershave still clung to the soft pink fabric. Too bad his desire for her had evaporated so quickly. A growl-like sound rose in his throat and he sat up and grabbed the gown from her hand.

At least he knew she was still in the room.

"John, I want a baby."

His eyes narrowed in a green ice stare. "Don't try to pull the baby thing." He tossed the gown at her. "Say your peace and get out. I have to get some sleep."

She pressed her knees to the bed frame and spoke in a whisper. "I know who will make my babies. Your sperm and my eggs." She laughed in delight when he grabbed her arm.

"I don't want to hear about sperm and eggs tonight, Flower." He tossed the sheet aside and sat up. "If you have something real to say, spit it out."

"Okay." Did he know his wonderful penis was on display, thick, wide and well veined and plush with a large silken head? "I'm going to be nice to you and make you want me again."

He snorted softly. "That's it?" He stood up and gripped her shoulders. "I've always wanted you, Bella." Reaching around her, he turned the light off and flopped back onto his bed. "Get out."

She stood in the dark for several minutes, quietly contemplating her next move. As if there had been no ugly words between them, she crawled up onto the bed and over him, dropping down to cuddle against his rear.

He reached around and pushed her hips away. Her grin widened and she sighed deeply, working her leg between his. Having sex would have been wonderful, but at the moment, she would settle for just his big hard body lying next to her. There was nothing as important as John, as him saying he wanted her back and that he loved her. She just didn't know how to make it happen.

* * * *

Bella found the room vacant of male company the next morning when she woke with a start. In her concern over getting into bed with John, she had forgotten to set her small alarm clock. Six AM and she had to shower and throw something together for a flight to New Orleans.

The aroma of coffee permeating the house was welcome and Bella hurried into the shower, lathering up and rinsing as quickly as possible. She left the shower, drying off as she hurried to the closet. It made no difference what she wore and the yellow silk suit her hand touched first would be fine. Luckily, she had hung the jacket over a sheer white blouse.

Her hair was a real bone of contention. It was still wet and hanging wild and heavy down her back. She considered cutting it off as she ran to the stack chest where she kept her undies.

Pulling out bras and panties, she threw them in the general

direction of her weekender. Of course getting dressed was a struggle that morning, even putting on her underwear caused her to huff with exertion. Damn getting up late. She hated it.

Dressed at last, she glanced in the mirror over the stack chest and grimaced. She knew her hair was a mess, but that couldn't be helped at the moment. The only good thing about her look was the nipped in jacket of the suit accentuating her waist and breasts. She figured that the skirt could be a bit shorter to tease John. A fold over to the waistband altered the length significantly.

As with most mornings, there wasn't enough time to tame her hair. She left it free to dry into coils and waves that careened over her shoulders and down her back. Worst case scenario, she would stuff it all under a nice hat. To be on the safe side, she took a lemon colored straw hat with a narrow brim from a box and laid it on her travel bag.

She started for the kitchen but ran back to the stack chest and pulled out a pair of lace and ribbon bedecked panties. She sprayed them with her perfume, smiling secretively while shoving them under John's pillow.

Before she walked down the hall toward the kitchen, she took a deep breath, preparing for whatever the next few minutes would bring.

Out in the kitchen, John sat at the counter, reading the morning paper and drinking coffee. She took a cup from the cupboard and filled it and then spooned in several sugars and a generous helping of cream. She took a sip before speaking to John.

"Good morning, lover."

He ignored her greeting and made lots of noise folding the paper. "Where will you be?"

"Read the list," she said in a singsong fashion. She patted his back and trailed her finger over his neck and let it slide into his ear.

He leaned away. "I'd rather you told me like an adult would."

"Okay." Bella walked around to the sink and peeled an orange, dropping the peel into the trash container. She took a deep breath and looked up at the ceiling like a kid reciting a poem. "I am being sent to New Orleans on assignment. A major find of rare books has been unearthed and has to be documented." She gazed at him with a patient smile.

His gaze revealed little interest in what she was saying. "Just make sure you show up here Monday morning."

"Would I disappoint you, gorgeous?"

She walked around the counter and stood behind him, leaning against him to grab a sweet roll. She pressed her breasts to him and closed her eyes, her lips issuing the softest sigh they could deliver. The subtle movement of his muscles told her she had left her imprint on him.

He gripped his paper in both hands, scowling at her when the shuttle arrived and the driver blew the horn.

"Tell your man out there to try and miss the mail box this time."

Bella sighed. She stopped trying to make up with him. It was too early and he was obviously horny and grumpy, but she didn't have time to properly seduce him. She grabbed her handbag and luggage, plopped the hat on her head and flounced her hips in his direction.

"Kiss my foot, John."

He turned to look at her as she opened the screen door. "No ass this time?"

Her laugh was ripe with devilment. "Sorry, lover. I don't have time."

* * * *

After Bella left, John lay across the counter and groaned. Damn if he didn't miss her already.

Loosening the knot in his tie, he stood and walked to the door to stare out at the roses on the fence. His gaze went to the garage and then slowly shifted to the windmill. How the hell had his life become some wild cartoon? He grunted in derision. All of his troubles started and ended with Flower.

He watched Roscoe as he happily chewed on the shoe Bella had thrown down from her perch, like some princess tossing bread to the poor at her feet.

That description fit him perfectly. He could be counted in the throng of people that let her screw them over and wipe her feet on them. He exhaled roughly. None of that was true. Bella usually was the recipient of dirty looks and envious remarks simply because she was gifted with looks and an unforgettable presence.

As for her screwing him over, he had asked for everything she threw his way. Anyway, they were not a couple. Yes, the sex was too unbelievable to describe and he liked being with her. Who was he trying to kid? He was crazy about her. But, he knew down the road she would tire of his homebody ways and long to find a new challenge. She couldn't help herself.

The other thing was the motorcycle. He couldn't believe she had sold the damn thing, but worse, he couldn't believe how furious he had been. He took the bottle of scotch from the refrigerator and snapped the cap off to take a swig.

Realizing he was acting like a wino, he put the bottle away and closed the back door. Nothing said he had to go to work today. So, he wouldn't.

Stripping down to his boxers, John pulled the comforter down to the foot of the bed and then plumped the pillows, planning to do some reading. The first thing to alert him to a trap was the fragrance of Bella. It came to him like a soft kiss.

He lifted the pillow off the bed and stared down at the female finery. Lace, ribbons and perfume all whispered little secrets about her.

Clasping the panties in his fist, he lay down and moaned. He should go on to work. But, if he did, Max would show up at the office and easily deduce some crisis was at work in the Lawless household. No way could he take laughing derision from that cantankerous old coot today.

Gazing at the handful of seduction in his fist, John decided he would not lie around and worry about what Flower planned to do to him in the future. He would meet that when it hit. Right now, he had something else to deal with.

He got out of bed and pulled on Levis and a dark blue T-shirt. After he got his boots on, he took his wallet and keys from the dresser and headed for the back door. He groaned and turned to stalk back into his room and shoved the panties under his pillow. Sure, he was a fool, but he would be lonesome without her tonight. Any port in a storm.

* * * *

Driving back into town, John decided to stop at the office to see if his loving spouse had called. The lobby receptionist gave him her trademark smile, sweet and innocent and dripping with sensual invitation. He gave her a little salute just like he had for the past three years and took the stairs up to his second floor office.

His secretary was busy at the word processor and barely looked up when he spoke to her. "My kind of woman."

He sat down behind his desk and looked over the stack of new contracts to be signed. Something the color of lilacs in his glass cigar humidor caught his eye. He lifted the lid and pulled out the lilac ribbon. "What the hell?" Something clanked against the glass container and he caught it in his fingers. A ring, and a damn expensive one at that.

Attached to the delicate ribbon was a tiny gift card. Carrying it to the window, he read the dainty printing. "To keep you safe while I am away. Lovingly yours, Bella Flower"

She must have stopped there before going to the airport. He grimaced hard, turning the great looking piece of jewelry over in his palm. His heart plummeted to his socks. Her ability to make him feel like a scum bag was so powerful he had almost been suckered in by the ring.

He'd totally forgotten her words, that she had used the sale money to buy him a ring. Damn it. It was a bauble to her, a trinket to reel him in. Apparently, Ms. Bella wasn't through messing with his head.

Now, why the hell did she want to tease a pitiful son of a bitch like him? And more to the point, why did he have a gnawing hunger for the hell cat, a hunger that grew in proportion each time they made love?

He walked back to his desk and hit the intercom button. "Helen, did Bella come by today?"

There was a rustle of papers first, then Helen's soft reply. "Lincoln was on security duty when she came in early this morning. Is there anything wrong?"

He exhaled and sat down in his chair. "No, Helen. Everything's fine."

Chapter Fifteen

The music was loud and the air stale. John sat at the end of the splintered oak bar and kept up small talk with the heavyweight bartender. Over the course of two hours, he had learned that the barkeep's name was Hog. The more beers he had, the less strange it sounded to hear Hog call him John Boy. The Atom Bomb Saloon was the fifth one he'd stopped at that day and frankly, he was getting a little tight. This was the last one today.

So far, he had learned that the bikers in the Bomb liked to race and were not much into the hardcore stuff like murder and mind altering drugs. At the moment, there were twenty of them gathered around a pool table, laughing and holding a guy upside down over a spittoon. A spittoon for Christ's sake.

John grinned at the horseplay in the back of the room. His mirth turned to hot curiosity when a huge biker strolled into the bar and more or less challenged any and all to race for money or iron. Iron meaning their bikes. John listened while a guy in patriotic red, white and blue leather spoke up, accepting the challenge. Tex was going to meet all comers Saturday morning at the old fairgrounds.

The bartender shook his head and grunted. "Tex just got that Indian and is taking everybody to the cleaners with it."

John swallowed his mouthful of beer and a good portion of air with it. He'd struck gold. "You say he has an Indian?"

"Yep. Said he picked it up out at some ranch from a cute little gal he would've liked to have brought home with him."

"That right?" John looked around the bar, trying to come up with something sensible. "Say, you know anyone in here that has a bike to sell?"

"Sure. All these bums have bikes for sale." The bartender grinned at him. "You thinking of racing Tex?"

Digging in his pocket, John pulled out several bills and tossed them on the bar to pay for his last beer. "Maybe. Just as soon as I get some wheels."

"Just so happens I have a real beauty out back and you don't have to buy her."

John chuckled, accustomed to attempted rip-offs by guys while he was in the Navy. "What's the catch?"

Leaning on the bar and talking low, the bartender explained his offer. "I can't ride no more. Busted hip and major heart problem. I just hate to see Black Beauty sit back there and let an old fart like Tex make her look bad." He slid another bottle of beer toward John. "You maybe want to race her for me?"

John was probably putting his ass in a sling, but he couldn't walk away. He rubbed his jaw and looked over the rowdy crowd.

The barkeeper jostled his elbow. "Well, what do ya say?"

There was the option of trying to buy the Indian back or go out and win it. Buying it didn't appeal to him. The damn bike was his and he wasn't about to pay for it again. "Okay." John smacked his palm down on the beer soaked bar. "I'm in. Show me Black Beauty."

"Hot damn." Hog shook John's hand and grinned like a kid. "Let's go look at her." With amazing agility, Hog hustled from behind the bar and out the back door with John in tow. Hog unlocked the door and then pointed inside. "There she is."

John nodded and walked over to look at the huge bike with tall handlebars. "She's a real beauty alright. Is she tuned up?"

Hog snorted. "Spend most of my life out here. She's cherry."

"She looks it." John straddled the leather seat and hugged his thighs to the mass of steel and rubber. "You sure you want to use this bike?"

"I ain't askin for anything if you lose. Just give that loud mouth a run for his money."

"I don't plan on losing." John leaned over the handlebars and shook Hog's hand. "I want that Indian."

He pushed the bike outside when Hog propped the door back. They stopped in the alley that led to a dirt service road. The bike started the old fashioned way. Muscle required. John got back on and then jumped on the starter pedal. One hop and she growled to life, sucking air in a furious roar as he worked the gears.

"Son of a bitch. What a feeling." He grinned and rode the bike around in tight circles before riding around to the front of the bar.

Tex stood outside, grinning confidently when John stopped in front of him. "You thinkin' about taken me on, man? That's Hog's bike, ain't it?"

John nodded. "Yep. I'm riding Hog's bike."

"You're on, boy." Tex grinned showing his big square teeth. "Plan on losin' your ass and Hog's bike."

"Yeah, Tex. I hope you're a good loser. I'm taking the Indian."

* * * *

Bella lifted the last case of documented books onto a shelf and wiped her forehead. The humidity in New Orleans was thick as soup. Her assigned partner for the job was Sara Wills and she worked fast and quietly. Bella liked that. She wanted to get back to Dallas.

Sara stopped working and looked at Bella. "Are these books worth so much sweat?" She dug in a tissue box for another handful and dabbed at her neck. "Dang, I'm melting."

Bella nodded and turned the fan on her companion. "Don't think about it, Sara. Let's hurry. Mr. Perkins wants us out of here by this evening."

"Can't be soon enough for me," Sara grumbled and went on with her work.

The two women conversed little and didn't take a lunch break, completing their assignment ahead of schedule.

Bella couldn't shake the feeling she was never going to get that once in a lifetime chance at an important find. "I'm going to ask for a better assignment when we get back to Dallas."

Where was her dig in Egypt? There were all kinds of sites in the American southwest. Why had she gone to school? Her mood was going straight to the bottom, but Sarah's suggestion pulled her out.

"Let's have dinner out of the hotel. Someplace with a bar."

They left the building and hailed a taxi that took them to a nice restaurant near their hotel. The place was packed and while they waited to be seated, the young women had a cocktail at the bar.

In the course of their chatting, Bella showed Sara her wedding ring. She bit the inside of her lip to keep syrupy feelings for John from overtaking her.

"You must be very happy," Sara said. "He obviously adores you."

Honesty stopped Bella from creating a rosy image of her marriage. "He's a rare find, all right."

She sipped her drink and glanced around the room at the crowd, not focusing on any one face.

Then she noticed him, a shiver of concern trickling over her. The stranger at the end of the bar stared at her and hoisted his drink when he caught her glance. He smiled. She shuddered and whispered to Sara. "Whoever he is, we don't want his company or his drink."

Sara made her feelings clear. "Could he look anymore like a cartoon rat?"

Bella groaned. "Oh, hell. Here he comes." She turned her head to avoid looking at him.

She was accustomed to men hitting on her. Sometimes it was flattering. Most of them were harmless, but none of them trustworthy according to Roman and Max. So far, their words of advice had proven true. This time was different. The man made her nervous.

She gave her full attention to her glass, but didn't miss the guy making his way over to stand beside her.

"Ma'am." He inclined his head toward her and Sarah. "You ladies work for the antiquities people?"

His question surprised Bella. "Who are you? I don't recall ever meeting you before."

"Oh, no, ma'am. We've never met." He bowed a little at the waist. "But I know some of the people employed at the library and they were nice enough to point you out to me. They said you were working here for a short time. That you were interested in really fine things."

She arched her brows and took note of his dark, sharp features. "How nice." The outdated sharkskin suit on his thin frame was interesting. "Is there anything else?"

He appeared apologetic. "Forgive my ignorance, ma'am. My name is Royal Port. As a matter of interest to you perhaps, I have connections to several national import/export dealers."

"Mr. Port, these things are not difficult to locate."

"Not like these dealers." He leaned into the narrow space between her and Sara.

"That's nice." She glanced at Sara who smiled patiently and grimaced when he pursued the conversation.

"It could be really nice for someone looking for the rare and unusual." He stuck a cigarette in the corner of his mouth and it bobbed up and down when he talked. I know where and when a plane of highly sought after plunder is landing."

Sara gripped Bella's arm and whispered, "He's too good to be true. Hard to resist though."

Bella ignored the whispered comment. "We're not on a buying trip, Mr. Port."

He waved his hand as if to dispel any suspicions she might have. "I'm not selling anything. I just know some groups that do sell high end items."

Bella had to admit to being curious. "Are these legal shipments?"

His eyes widened. "I'm not privy to any information like that. But these dealers have everything from King Richard's commode to tea pots from London to Scotland."

The man's words struck a powerful note of longing and hope in Bella's heart. "What would your friends have from Scotland?"

He took a small notebook from his pocket and flipped through its worn pages. "Linen, lace, china, crystal and silver. What catches your fancy?"

Bella waved her hand to stop him. "No, I'm not looking for anything in particular. Unless..." She cut her answer short.

He leaned in to smile at Bella. "You have a particular item on your wish list? Lace or fine linen?"

"Neither." She accepted the embossed business card he held out to her. "I'm not interested in mid-list items, Mr. Port. I would be curious to see anything to do with royal wedding items. From Scotland, sixteen-hundred era."

He wrote furiously while she spoke and replaced the notebook back in his pocket. "One way to find out. I'll contact them and make an appointment for you to meet my colleagues in a day or so."

She shook her head. "I'm leaving tomorrow evening."

"I'm sure they would be more than happy to call you at your home. Where did you say you were from?"

Sure they would, and get John all over her rear for dealing with undesirables. "I didn't." Bella saw Sara's scowl of disapproval. What were her choices? Risk giving him her phone number and maybe get the wedding goblets, or just lots of obscene calls? Well, hell. It was her neck and her phone. She wanted what was rightfully hers.

She'd take the chance. After scribbling her cell phone number on a blank slip of paper, she handed it to Royal Port. "Have your associates call me if they have authentic pieces from that time period."

He put the paper in his pocket and bowed slightly. "As you wish, ma'am."

He left then, disappearing into the crowd. Bella grimaced as a twinge of worry whispered in her ear. "I can't call John this time," she mumbled.

Chapter Sixteen

John knew when Bella arrived home the night before. She made enough noise to raise the dead after the airport shuttle bus dropped her at the door. Now, here he was, bone tired after missing hours of sleep, getting ready for work while she snored in his bed.

He eyed the sleeping princess' trail of clothing strewn about the room. Looked like Roscoe had made a raid after she had retired. A pair of pale pink panties were snagged on a nail head in the terrace doorway and one tan sandal that had died a painful death now rested on the bathroom floor, missing all its straps.

Taking care not to disturb her friend Roscoe's work, John decided to wake Bella. "Paybacks are hell," he mumbled, yanking the quilt off her. His enjoyment was short-lived. She rolled onto her stomach and stretched. She was bare butt naked, looking smooth and delicious.

He smacked the bottom of her foot. "Rise and shine, Flower."

She searched for the quilt without opening her eyes and groaned. "Go away, John."

He pulled on her foot. "Not today, Bella. The board meeting." He finished buttoning his shirt and pulled his jacket on. "You have twenty-nine minutes to get ready and get there."

Her reply was muffled in the pillows. "Ready for what?"

"Your first board meeting."

She sat upright and covered her face with both hands. "My God, I can't. I'm too tired and I'm dizzy."

"I'll vouch for that." Too late, he realized the comment had pierced her armor. She gazed at him as if he was a disease.

It just had always been so easy, the way they talked to each other and even now since he was still mad as hell at her. But he wasn't going to treat her like a baby, even if she was one. "Stop bellyaching. You wouldn't be so sleepy if you had gone to bed when you got home."

He loved the image she presented. Sleep warmed and birds nest hair made her almost irresistible. Almost.

"How would you know what I did?" She yawned and glared at him with her sleep swollen eyes and puffy, lush lips. "While you were snoring, I had something on my mind."

He looked at the ceiling and counted to ten. She was leaving herself wide open for zingers. But, no. He would control himself. "It's your choice. Get up, get dressed and ride in with me, or sack out. I don't care which you choose."

Something whistled past his head and hit the wall. "Damn it, Bella." He saw the disemboweled clock that at one time sat on his nightstand, rolling about the room in a jillion pieces.

"No, you go to hell, you tight assed son of a bitch." She ran to the closet and yanked something out and ran to search around in her luggage that she hadn't put away. "Stop looking at me. You aren't the hired boy anymore, so keep your distance."

He felt the full impact of what his attitude had wrought. She was hurt and that meant he was to suffer until she decided he'd had enough. Only thing was, he didn't give a damn. "If you're ready to go in fifteen minutes, you can ride with me."

"Get out, you pompous asshole. I wouldn't be seen with you in town. People might think we're together."

* * * *

John didn't know how she did it, but Bella strode out of the bedroom and down the hall to the kitchen in sixteen minutes. She grabbed her handbag and a bagel off the counter and walked outside after kicking the screen door open.

"Bella, the Jeep's over here."

He may as well have spoken to Roscoe who trotted after her. Bella went to her little red sports car and got in without looking back at him. He couldn't help but grin as the crafty little herding dog jumped in the front seat with her and appeared to be ready for a joyride.

John's grin froze on his lips when Bella threw her car into reverse and backed up until her bumper was inches from his Jeep. He could swear she was flipping him the bird as she tore down the drive toward the highway.

He followed Bella down the lane, or rather, her dust trail, until she pulled over at the entrance of the driveway. She opened the passenger side door and Roscoe jumped out. He ran back toward the house with his tail wagging.

The brief stop for doggie pampering had put him a few minutes behind schedule. He gave her the lead, figuring he wouldn't take the chance of making her any madder. They drove into the Cantatore Brokerage Firm's parking garage and John gave her plenty of room to maneuver into a parking space.

Glad to sit back and watch her get out of her car, he sat in the Jeep while she sashayed past him without looking his way.

What a knockout. Bella starred in her own private movie with every gesture and breath she took. Dressed in a white flowery mini skirt and a sleeveless white cotton blouse, she looked every inch the mega sexpot. Somewhere between the ranch and Dallas, she had pinned her hair up in a fancy knot. He eyed the chopstick ornaments jammed in the gleaming twist. Damn things could be lethal to an unwary male. He grinned and climbed out of the Jeep, following his unpredictable wife.

Dutifully, he hurried to open the door for her, looking into her eyes and grinning. "Excuse me, ma'am." He grabbed for the brass door handle and covered her hand with his. "May I get that for you?"

Her gaze scalded him. "You can get lost."

"Thank you, ma'am. After you, ma'am."

She scowled and looked skyward, jerking her hand free and shouldering past him. As she hurried up the short flight of steps, John eyed the curve of her hips and wondered if her inner thighs were still ticklish.

After all these years, he still foamed at the mouth over her.

His pleasant thoughts were terminated at the door of the conference room. Bella walked in like a commando with her self-confident choice of chairs at the head of the table. She gazed around at the twenty pairs of eyes locked on her.

John leaned over her shoulder and murmured. "Good choice, ma'am." He took the chair beside her and opened his briefcase. "Gentlemen, shall we get started?"

After the initial round of small talk and the rustle of papers, the meeting began and John took a moment to look at Bella. Ten minutes into the meeting and she was making it clear she was dangerously bored.

Obviously, the monotone reading of a multi-paged bylaws change lulled her into a near coma. At least that was what she wanted him to think. Her lips turned up slightly at the corners while her lids lowered to show him she was sleepy.

"Flower." He leaned against her shoulder and murmured softly. "Would you like some coffee?"

"I'll have one of those jelly donuts, too." She licked her lips and yawned.

"Fine." John poured her coffee and handed her a plate with one donut on it.

"Two please." Her smile was stingy

"Of course." He wondered what kind of crap she had planned for him now. He should kick her out of the office, chair, donuts and all. She yawned again, looking a lot like a baby hippo.

It was time for the first vote and he wasn't sure what had been said. Damn it. He had to get his mind off the devil's daughter and worry about his real life. Fate conspired against him. It was a tied vote.

"Bella." He waited while she licked at a dab of jelly on her lips. "Bella."

"What?"

"The board has reached a tied vote. You're required to vote."

She smiled at him and it wasn't a loving one. "How did he vote?"

"Are you referring to me, Bella?"

She brushed her knee against his under the table. "How did you vote?" She opened her handbag and pulled out a lipstick.

John looked around the room at the faces of the shareholders and fought the urge to choke her.

They looked as messed up by her actions as he felt. He was damn tired of feeling confused and weak in her most supreme presence. He was fed up with her antics.

"Gentlemen, excuse us." He caught her arm in a controlling grip and pulled her from the chair. Her mouth opened and he hissed, "Can it."

For once he had surprised her, rendering her temporarily speechless. But, as he propelled her out the door and down the hallway, he caught her look of enjoyment. She was loving it.

He clenched his jaw and growled at her. "This way, Flower." He stifled a groan and escorted her around a corner toward a door at the end of a narrow hallway.

"This is so sudden." She let her shoulder slouch and tried to lean on him. "Just where are you taking me?"

He opened the door to a small utility room. "Inside."

She walked past him and her perfume beckoned as he followed her in and closed the door. Her comment caught him off guard.

"You must want in my pants awfully bad." In the light coming through the frosted windowpane of the door, he could see the devil leaping in her eyes. He reached for the light switch. She caught his arm. "Don't turn the light on."

He was finished. Her presence penetrated his skin and went deep in his soul. *Just one more time, Lord. I won't ask for another thing. Just one more time.*

What did her lips taste like? He had forgotten. Were her arms really so strong, yet tender? And her whisper of desire for him couldn't have been as beautiful as he thought. Just once more.

She didn't move to avoid his touch, or brush his hand off when he toyed with the ornament in her hair.

"Bella." He pulled the sticks from her hair one by one and let her hair slide over his fingers. "I'm glad you're home."

Her voice slipped over his ears like a shot of smooth whiskey. "Then show me."

Whatever life had planned for him, nothing could top this moment. She leaned back against the towels and slid her arms around his waist, pulling him to her. He couldn't help being mush in her hands, or getting granite hard just feeling the warmth of her hips.

"You were right, Flower. I do want in your pants."

"Let me show you where they are." She guided his hand to the warmth between her legs and forced his fingers inside her panties, moving against them. "Use your sonar, handsome."

"I've never had a sexy wingman before, baby." He pressed his free hand against the wall behind her.

"You wasted a lot of time. I've always liked great big sailors." She gasped and bucked against him as he pushed her panties aside and slid his finger into her warmth.

"I'm making up for it now." He looked into her eyes and saw everything she was feeling. White-hot passion meant for him. He bent down to nuzzle her throat and nudged her chin up to cover her lips with his. He wondered if he was upside down after her tongue darted in and out of his mouth, teasing his until it was hard, just like his cock.

Right now, he admitted to himself that she turned him into a codfish every time he touched her little secret. "You're slick and hot and I'm in a meltdown mode."

"I lube just for you." She unzipped his slacks and closed her fingers around him, pulling his erection free and squeezing him in her palm. "Let's go at it. I'm about to climax."

His arms shook as he pressed her back against the linen and raised her butt up to wedge in between her thighs. She clasped his waist with her legs and lifted her hips, guiding him into her center and clamped her muscles around him in a possessive action. He lurched forward in reflex as the floor seemed to drop away from under his feet.

She moaned deep in her throat and his blood became a bubbling brew of nitro and lava.

Dangerous was how he felt, thrusting into his woman while he plunged his tongue in her sweet witch's mouth. Her lips pulsed with his and suckled his tongue, her teeth nipping his lips until he tasted blood.

How deep could he go, how much could he take from her supple, accepting body and keep his sanity? Bella demanded every inch and pound of him, leaning her head back to sob out her need for more.

"John, don't stop now, not ever." She gripped his hair and pulled his head down to suck on his earlobe, biting until he groaned in pain. "Make me come," she sobbed out. "I need you."

He pushed into her until he heard her gasps of rapturous release and felt her love nectar hot and wet around him. He forgot how big he was and his strength as he drove into her, feeling the power of and savoring being one with his Flower. With a final steely stroke, he climaxed, coming to full awareness to find he was wrung out and tired enough to sag against her.

His ears rang with remnants of straining he had been through with his smiling bride. Christ, she was being so sweet right now he just wanted to make her come again. But that was not going to happen, not when he heard voices echoing down the hallway.

"Aw, damn it." He kissed her hungrily and let her go. "Stand still. I'll get what you need."

He grabbed several washcloths from a shelf and turned the hot water on in the deep sink, loading the cloths up with liquid soap. He wrung them out and handed one to Bella.

He reeled from shock at being in a water closet, washing his cock and watching Bella remove her underwear and clean up. It was just too much like a sex dream for him to comprehend. His life was on a tilt of bad choices and this was his dumbest move ever. Screwing in a closet at work, while the board waited.

She handed him her washcloth and picked up her panties from the floor. With a soft smile and sigh, she dropped them in her handbag. If she didn't keep her legs together, the stockholders might die of heart attacks.

"I think we better get out of here before the janitor wants in." He kissed the top of her head while they washed their hands, side by side, hip to hip. She drove him to do irrational things, but damn, he was certifiably nuts over her. They shared a hand towel.

"John, have you ever made it in a closet before?"

"No, and I'm glad my first time was with you."

He checked the front of his slacks and zipped them up. She grinned and patted his member.

"You look sexy the way you are. Don't get rid of all the evidence."

He grinned and raked his fingers through his hair. "We still have to go back in there, Bella."

Her eyes widened and she touched her hair that hung in a knot of curls and tangles. "Oh, hell."

She found her hair ornaments and quickly twisted her hair back up in a messy knot. "How's that?"

"Perfect." He fastened her blouse and wiped a smudge of mascara from her cheek. "I'll go out first."

He opened the door and stepped out. The hall was empty until Bella came through the door. His secretary rounded the corner and pulled up short when she saw him and Bella.

"You two are wanted in the conference room and pronto." The

usually stoic woman grinned.

"Family business comes first, I always say."

Bella smiled and straightened her skirt. "You can tell them we are on our way."

Catching her arm, John gave her a speculative smile. "Okay, Bella. We had our good time in the closet, but that probably doesn't change a thing. Does it?"

"Not a thing."

He followed her back into the conference room filled with curious stockholders and went down in defeat when she voted. After the meeting adjourned, Bella left, going to her own job and leaving him to make hard decisions and face the grim reality of the fast approaching finale in their relationship.

Chapter Seventeen

The afterglow of their tryst lasted only until she got home that evening. Instead of being in the den working on some new deal, John was in the bedroom.

"You're packing?" Fear touched her heart. She wanted him to stay with her, at least for that night. "Where are you going?"

He looked up and motioned to his briefcase laying on the bed. "Yeah, got a meeting in New York."

"When did you make these plans? And airline tickets?" She grew ill with unreasonable jealousy over an unknown competitor. "New York is awfully far away"

"I'm going in the company plane." He laughed and moved her aside to look in a dresser drawer. "Why the sudden concern with my whereabouts?" He grabbed several changes of underwear and shirts from the drawers and put them in his duffle bag.

When he took three pairs of slacks from the closet, she blurted out in desperation.

"You don't need more than one change of clothing for one night."

"I didn't say it was an overnight. I'll be back the day after tomorrow."

"Oh. I wasn't being nosey, just was surprised that you were leaving." Why had she let herself sound like a fishmonger? She quieted her voice. "You hadn't mentioned a trip."

"It slipped my mind." He stopped moving around the room and took her arm, drawing her close. "Now listen, Bella." He touched her chin with his fingertip. "We might as well get used to being apart. We can't live together after the divorce proceedings are started."

"Where did that come from?" She pulled her arm from his grasp.

"What do you mean?" He spread his hands in a show of exasperation. "We both knew it was coming." He threw his slacks in the direction of his luggage.

He had hurt her before, but that was when she didn't know how deeply she loved him or that she couldn't live without him. It hadn't meant so very much before, but now, he simply ripped her heart out and stomped on it.

She pressed her palm to her midriff and tried to cover the ache that grew there. "You know you don't have to go on with this so-called marriage." She cringed when her voice broke. "I think I should go back to my apartment."

"And I told you I would stay till the end." He closed his duffle bag. "Or are you so dense you're willing to give up Roman's money because of your damn stubborn streak?" He pointed his finger at her nose. "And while we are being honest and open, just how much fun did you have making me think you were down on my level, broke and needing help?"

Bella took a ragged breath and walked away from him. "It seemed like a terrible waste of effort to go into all that since you hated me so much. I didn't want your pity then and I want it less now."

John picked up his luggage and carried it to the door. "I don't pity you and I don't want you to move out." He moved his hand and his keys jingled softly. "Why do that now? We'll see how things shake out in the coming weeks."

She couldn't speak through her numb lips and she shook her head instead. He stepped back inside the room and kissed the corner of her mouth and then left.

Hearing his footsteps carrying him away might as well have been stabs in her breast. She had lost him. No, she had never had him. She whispered a mournful farewell and went to the lonely room that would be hers until New Years day.

The rapture from the closet had an extremely short life. Bella was familiar with loneliness. What she felt now was deeper than a mere longing. It crushed her heart and desire to breathe. John didn't want her. She had to face up to it. No amount of wishing or sex would hold him.

Hurt and fearful of losing him, she wandered from room to room, remembering the good and bad times. She huffed. "Mostly bad times, you idiot, and mostly your fault."

She went to the kitchen and took a banana flip from the freezer. A soft whine made her open the screen door and Roscoe trotted in. The affectionate little dog followed her around the room and gazed at her with sad eyes. "Roscoe, you probably know I have made a fat mess of my life." She sat down on the floor beside him and hugged his neck while they shared the frozen cake.

The phone rang and Bella jumped to her feet to answer it. "John?"

The voice on the line scraped over her nerves. Royal Port identified himself.

"Ms. Cantatore?"

Relief washed over her. She had given him her card with her maiden name on it. "Mr. Port. Yes, I remember you."

"The business contacts we spoke of in New Orleans have a new shipment anchored off San Padre Island, if you're interested."

She chewed on her thumbnail in indecision. She worried this man was a crook, and possibly dangerous. Do it or not? She had to do it. "I am interested, Mr. Port. How do I identify the dealers from all the other boats out there?"

He made a wheezing sound and excused himself. "The boat is of the fishing variety. Bright blue and named The Virgin."

Bella forced her throat closed against her laugh. "Okay, how will I identify myself? I don't want to get shot for getting too close."

"I have given them a description, Ms. Cantatore. The boat will drop anchor in Blue Beach Cove three days from now, and only stay there for two nights." He paused then added, "Bring cash only."

"That is too risky." She frowned, having second thoughts about going. "I don't think so."

"I was told the cargo contains several extremely rare pieces from Scotland. Frankly, they are stolen from thieves that specialize in those types of artifacts. Very old and very beautiful."

She couldn't hesitate any longer. "Tell them I'll be there in time."

"Good. Register at the Blue Beach Inn."

"Is that enough? How will they know I am there?"

"They'll know."

"Oh." She heard the phone click. "That makes sense," she told Roscoe who thumped his tail on the floor.

She looked up when Ellie yoo-hooed through the screen door.

"Hey, Bella." Ellie wiped her brow and laughed. "I don't see you or John much. You been busy?"

"Yeah, you know with us working different hours, we try not to wake each other up." Bella stepped out onto the patio. "I'm going on an assignment in a couple of days. I'll be gone at least overnight."

"Lucky you, getting to go all the time to exciting, glamorous places."

Bella sighed. "It's not so great sometimes."

The two women chatted briefly before Ellie took Roscoe and went home to Buck. Bella hated the twinge of jealousy she felt over the other woman's good fortune.

Wiping everything from her thoughts but the boat off the shore of San Padre, Bella gathered up a change of clothes and her toothbrush and dropped them in a weekender. She checked to make sure she had several credit cards and her bank card. It would take several stops at ATMs to get enough money to buy what she hoped the dealers had.

Feeling way too small and inadequate, Bella crawled into John's bed and burrowed into his pillows.

* * * *

John wondered if he would ever get back to Dallas. He was ready to hear a meadowlark out in a pasture instead of a freaking siren. New York was fine, but Dallas was where Bella was.

"Bella Flower," he called out as he walked inside the house. "I'm home."

Silence greeted him and it was unsettling. An intense emptiness shot through him.

"Bella."

He looked around the kitchen and found a cake wrapper on the counter. The scrap of paper made him feel better, indicating her presence. Most of the lights were on. She must have been scared last night. The grandfather clock in the entry hall chimed. He groaned in contempt of his stupidity. It was too early for Bella to be out of bed.

As he walked through the rooms, something just didn't feel right in the house. He went around turning off lamps and looking in corners like a spooked kid. A sliver of worry lodged in his heart. She wasn't in either bedroom. Bella wasn't in the house.

He tried to remain calm, even nonchalant about where she might be. His gaze fell on a sheet of the fancy notepaper she used to doodle on while she talked on the phone. What in the hell did 'Blue Virgin' mean? He couldn't be calm while he worried about her. He was reaching for his keys when Ellie appeared at the kitchen door.

He palmed the keys and spoke to her.

"Ellie, I guess Bella had to leave early this morning?"

She nodded and held up a covered dish. "Yeah, I heard the airport shuttle pick her up about two hours ago. Roscoe always whines when she's leaving."

John conceded to himself, he felt the same way. "She didn't write it on the list. She always leaves one for me." Had he sounded worried? Well, damn it, he was. About what exactly, he wasn't sure.

Ellie opened the screen and handed him the dish she had been holding. "Good crisp bacon and omelet for you." She started to leave but paused. "You worried about her? She told me she had a new assignment last night."

"I don't suppose she said where it was."

"Nope." She patted his arm. "She'll call you and you'll feel better. Me and Buck are going for a ride up in the hills for a few hours. I'll see you later."

John set the dish on the stove and watched Ellie trot off, leaving him to wonder where Bella was. He had planned to fix her breakfast in bed and try to explain what he had only touched on the last time they talked. He remembered her hurt expression. Would he ever stop being the reason she cried?

* * * *

The night had been a long and sleepless one for John. By the time the sun had climbed over the hills in the east, he was making a second pot of coffee.

After it finished brewing, he took the pot and a cup out to the patio and sat on the glider. Too damn quiet. The quiet had never bothered him before Bella. His heart sagged, too full of loneliness to enjoy the daybreak.

He sat for another minute, his eyes adjusting to the soft blue-gray morning light. The garage door was open. "How prophetic," he muttered. The gaping door brought up vivid memories of his bike and Bella. "As usual, Lawless, you proved yourself to be a fool."

He understood her hurt and his parents' anger with him. He just didn't know if he could untangle the reasons he had been so upset with Bella. He still wanted his Indian and in a few hours, he would bring it home. He would deal with the other demon then.

That damn bike would be back in the garage and he wouldn't mention it to Bella. He'd been insensitive enough. Feeling better than he had for a long while, he got up and went in the house. While he showered and dressed, plans took shape on what his racing strategy would be.

He went out the door and bypassed his Jeep. Today he needed the ranch truck. He got in and turned the key in the ignition. The motor stuttered, and then kicked into a noisy rumble. His extra key for the Indian pressed against his thigh where it nestled in his jeans pocket. As he drove away from the house, he caught sight of Roscoe, lying on his back, playing with one of Bella's shoes.

Thirty minutes later, he was parked in front of The Bomb. He shook his head, noting at least fifty bikes parked around the building. They were waiting for him, positive he would either not show up or get lost in Tex's dust.

"Hell with that," he mumbled, getting out of the truck. John squared his shoulders and went inside the bar, speaking to Hog as he straddled a stool near the door. The bartender slid a foam topped mug his way.

"That'll clear your pipes out, John Boy."

John compared this morning to some he had spent in the Navy. "Thanks, Hog." He downed half the beer and wiped his mouth. "Really hit the spot." In reality he wanted to gag. His belly wasn't accustomed to warm booze before daybreak, or a blanket of smoke, tobacco and other things that were illegal.

He finished his beer as quickly as he could, looking around for his competition. He didn't have to look far. Tex busted in through the door, wearing a complete ensemble of black leather. He wore his big-toothed grin and hollered at John.

"I'll be damned. You did show up."

John stood and laughed, palming the keys to Black Beauty that Hog dropped into his hand. "Get ready. You're going to lose a lot more than a hundred bucks."

The bar exploded into a loud laughing party of taunts and backslapping among the bikers. They were ready for action. Hog grinned at John and punched him on the shoulder.

"Make me proud, boy."

What a way to start the day—lungs full of smoke and beer sloshing around in his empty gut. John wished now that he had eaten the bacon and eggs Ellie had brought to the house. Too late now. If he barfed, these toads would never let him live it down.

The crowd stumbled and shoved their way outside to get their bikes. Hog jerked his thumb in the direction of the alley. John nodded and walked around the corner of the building where the bike was parked. He mounted the bike, turned the key in the ignition and jumped on the starter pedal. The rumbling sound was music to his ears. If his gut would settle down, he would start having some fun.

"Let's go, John Boy."

The taunting voice belonged to Tex. John rode out to the street and made a sweeping gesture along with a sardonic smile. "What's the hold up, Tex?"

The race had already started as far as the crowd was concerned. They crowded John and Tex as they rode out to the old fairgrounds and in general caused a ruckus. The race was laid out and the two men shook hands. Whoever showed up alive from the old cattle shoots would be the winner. Two miles of ruts and mud holes shouldn't be too much for a hard ass like him.

John gazed at the Indian. From somewhere, a wisp of wind crossed his cheek much like Bella's little teasing trick.

Bella.

He was stung with the depth of his longing for her with his body and soul. And here he was out in a cow pie filled pasture trying to regain something he had lost quite honorably. It hadn't been his fault and sure as hell wasn't hers. He had been hanging on to that noisy plaything to reassure himself of his manhood. Bullshit. He wasn't half the man she deserved.

"Let's get at it, Tex. I have to get the Indian home and give her a bath."

The men rode in silence to the cattle shoots and then positioned themselves for the start. Hog would fire a pistol as the signal. Tex grinned at him and spit on the ground. John smiled and geared his bike up. A gunshot blasted through the calm of morning and the race was on.

Using every trick he knew, John tried to lose Tex, but the giant guy in black stayed next to him. The road conditions were hazardous at best, pocked with deep ruts and mud holes. He glanced over at Tex and the big grin on his competitor's face was like a slug to the unsettled gut and John knew Tex was already declaring himself the winner. So be it.

John muscled his way by Tex, getting a charge from the wind slapping him in the face and the rumble of two good engines. He could see a rut in the road that would have swallowed a child and went left of it. Tex didn't fare so well, bouncing in and out of the pit, he struggled to keep an upright position.

Elation born of certain victory filled John's sails as he flew down the narrow dirt road. He turned his head and watched Tex right his bike and gain on him. Relaxing his grip on the throttle, he let Tex blow by him.

In that moment, he realized he didn't want or need that piece of cold metal. He wanted and needed Bella. Clenching his jaws, he let his bike slow, grimacing as Tex blew by him.

Opening up the speed again, he gave chase to Tex who lifted his fist to show John the race was won. In the distance, the biker gang waited, yelling insults at both men as they roared across the finish line formed by beer cans.

John shook his head and navigated several donuts in front of the bar. He got off Hog's bike and pushed it to the side of the building, then went back to where Tex waited. He held his hand out.

"You'll be needing this extra set of keys. Good race, man."

"This was your ride? You need to learn how to gear down, John Boy." Something like a gleam of challenge flickered in Tex's eyes. "Wouldn't want to race again, would you?"

"Nope. I'd just win it back. It's caused me to make a lot of bad choices." He gripped the handlebars. "You enjoy it."

Tex laughed and handed John the key. "Hell yeah. I'd be glad to race you for her anytime."

"Don't make any plans on it." John turned to clap Hog on the shoulder. "I'll get the bike back, Hog."

"Aw hell, John Boy." Hog looked down at his dusty boots. "I don't want the thing and I'll settle up with Tex. And you're better off without the Indian. Damned things have ruined a lot of good men. Hey, come on back once in a while."

Later, as he drove toward the ranch, John tried to ignore the deep melancholy that settled over him. He groaned with impatience, knowing full well the cause of his dissatisfaction was dread of the huge vacancy Bella would leave in his life when she divorced him.

He got out of the truck and walked toward the house.

Waiting for him was Roscoe, looking pretty damn melancholy. "What do you want from me, mutt? I miss her, too." He leaned down and patted the dog's head. "Get used to being lost without her is my best advice. It's a hazard of being in love with the Flower."

Chapter Eighteen

For the tenth time in an hour, Bella peered out through the grimy window of the small motel room she had rented. The Blue Beach Inn was an out of the way place and sat near the beach in a grove of scrub trees and rocks. All in all, she found it disgusting and frightening.

The room wasn't air conditioned, but she hesitated to go outside the room. Through a tear in the window shade, she watched couples come and go past her unit. They appeared to be drunk and openly fondled one another as they walked along. The crowd on the beach got noisier as time passed.

She tried to be patient, waiting for the dealers to contact her. She had registered under her maiden name. Now, all she could do was wait. Concern tugged at her as she looked out at the desolate cove where the Blue Virgin was supposed to be anchored. There was nothing on the water, not even a sailboat.

The sun had set. Fires burned on the beach and the noise increased. She heard women laughing and screaming and men yelling and cussing. All that was mixed with the sound of shattering glass. "Oh, yeah. Party time," she mumbled.

Her hands trembled when she tried to repair the tattered window shade with chewing gum and checked the lock on her door. Worry strained her nerves and she began to think about one thing. Getting home.

She slid her cell phone under the bed, keeping it handy if she got a call. She laughed at herself, realizing no one knew where she was except undesirables.

Before she could straighten up, the door to her room exploded under the vicious kick of a hooded man. He ran inside the room, followed by four other men in hoods. They all began shouting at her, pushing her off the bed.

She screamed and was pulled several feet when the tallest man grabbed her by the hair. He slapped her several times when she screamed again. "Shut up, whore." He twisted her hair around his wrist and yelled in her contorted face. "Where's the money, your credit cards, jewelry?"

He didn't wait for her answer, but tore her wristwatch from her arm and broke her crucifix and chain from her neck. She screamed in pain as her hoop earrings were viciously pulled from her ears.

She clawed at the foul smelling man's wrist and fought to stand up. Natural instinct to survive forced a shrill scream from her throat, which earned her another blow across the neck.

One from the group walked to where she struggled on the floor and touched the front of his greasy trousers. "Shut up or I'll stick this down your throat."

She clenched her teeth and continued to struggle against the fist in her hair. "Take the money," she gasped, "and get out."

Her tormenters laughed in unison. "Bitch, we're taking your shit alright, but we ain't leaving until we fuck you through the floor." The men all laughed and spewed filthy comments.

She decided to fight for her life. Her scream shrilled out through the shattered door and seemed to startle the men. They were occupied ransacking her property. The slap she received for her outburst tripled her effort to draw blood from her captor's arm and hand with her nails. His grunt made her think of a smelly swine. He kicked her in the side.

Her eyes were closed and tears streamed down her bruised cheeks, but Bella refused to wail. She heard things falling and glass breaking all around her while the hoods searched the place. She opened her eyes and saw one of the thugs with her handbag and another searching her luggage.

After they took her cash and credit cards, they turned their attention on her.

"Okay, whore. You probably ain't never had a man before, so now you gonna get five at once."

Her captor let go of her hair for an instant and she tried to crawl toward the door. She was kicked again by a laughing thug. One grabbed her arm, yanking hard and crushing her hand in a vise-like grip to pull her wedding ring from her finger. Her brain cried out to her—*scream, Bella, scream!*

She opened her mouth and forced the sound from her lungs, flailing out with her feet and baring her teeth against the group. She kept it up until she couldn't breathe and her fight weakened under the feral attack to her body as the thugs tried to spread her legs and arms.

"John," she cried and fought her attackers. She raged against them and the darkness that hovered over her. She gulped in the cool air that rushed around her and screamed as firm hands touched her. "No, don't touch me."

Someone yelled at her from very far away. "Lady, you okay?"

She couldn't speak, but nodded, opening her eyes to gaze up at the faces of strangers, a man and a woman. "Are they gone?" She shrank away from his touch and frantically looked around the room.

The woman smoked her cigarette in big hard puffs and pointed to the door. "Somebody called the law and an ambulance. I hear a siren now."

There was noise and confusion and sirens and more shouting outside. For a split second, Bella was afraid the thugs were coming back and tried to get up but fell onto her knees.

The woman patted her on the shoulder. "Relax, honey. They ran like cowards when we got here. You okay? Got anyone to call?"

Bella sat up and gazed around. She wanted to curl up and bawl for a very long time, but scrambled to reach her cell phone. It felt like a lifeline in her hand. "Yes." Tears washed down her cheeks as she cried silently. "I've got someone to call."

* * * *

John had been in the sunroom when he heard the phone ring and bolted through the door to snatch up the receiver. He knew instinctively who it was.

"Bella?"

He heard her sob and then her voice.

"John."

Her voice sounded as if she was terrified and had broken as she began to sob out her explanation. He stopped her because he couldn't understand her. "Bella, honey. What's going on?"

He stumbled over a hassock and gripped the back of the sofa to steady himself. "Talk to me, Flower. Slowly. I'm listening."

Seconds passed and she finally let her words tumble out. "I'm in San Padre. John, will you come and get me? Please?" She was sobbing harder. "Please, John?"

He gripped the phone, imagining every horror known to man assaulting Bella. He'd never heard her cry like this before, not even when she'd had the hell scared out of her. "Bella, try to stop crying and tell me exactly where you are, okay?"

He could hear her gulping for breath before she answered him. "It's called the Blue Beach Inn." She immediately fell into tears again. "I wanted to buy the wedding goblets my parents were bringing home when they died, John." More sobs followed and then a telling statement. "He didn't come here like he promised."

"He, who?" John winced with anger and his skin burned with desire to hurt whoever caused her to be afraid. "Tell me you are okay, Bella."

"John, they broke into my room and hit me and took everything." She sobbed harder. "They hit me. So hard."

Hit her! Rage exploded in him to the point his ears pounded with the rush of his rampaging blood. "I'm on my way, Bella. If you're safe where you are, stay there. Tell me you're okay. Do you hear me?"

He could hear her blowing her nose and a woman's voice in the background. Then her voice again.

"I will, John. Please don't forget me."

Her plea cut him to shreds and he wanted to heave with guilt. When had she begun to doubt he would do anything for her if he was able to breathe at all? If his luck held, after tonight, she would never have reason to doubt him again.

* * * *

The small private businessmen's airport outside Dallas had been busy with weekend traffic and John could barely control his desire to be in the air. He wanted to bypass the chatter from the control tower. He agonized over what he considered a waste of time while the hired pilot gave the controller his flight plan. John bit back his impatient comments that they were moving too slow and settled into the co-pilots seat of the corporate helicopter.

He ignored the pilot's knowing grin while he checked his map a dozen times and re-checked the area of his destination with a buddy over his cell phone, and he sweat bullets while waiting for the tower to give them clearance to take off. After what seemed like hours, the chopper was in the air and they were on their way to San Padre and the Blue Beach Inn. He groaned audibly when he thought of the stinking description of the place his buddy had given him.

Halfway there, he dialed Bella's cell phone number. "You doing okay, Flower?" His heart resumed beating when she spoke to him.

"I'm okay, but please hurry."

"Almost there, baby. Just stay put and listen for the chopper. I want you to come outside when you hear it." He barely understood her answer. "Bella, I'll be there." The phone went dead and he prayed it had only been a bad connection.

They flew down the coast until the island was in sight and headed for the cove where the Blue Beach Inn was supposed to be. The shoreline was well marked with a succession of bonfires and neon lights on small buildings.

They hovered over the deserted camping area and prepared to set the chopper down. Loose paper and flimsy chairs were caught in the updraft and spun wildly before crashing back to the ground. Getting back on solid ground seemed to take a hell of a long time in his impatient frame of mind.

He motioned to the pilot to stay put, freed himself from the safety harness and jumped out onto the sandy campsite. Expecting trouble, he secured the revolver tucked in the waistband of his Levis and walked quickly across the deserted volleyball court.

There was nothing going on and that made him edgy. Where was everybody? He was sure there had been plenty of action there a few minutes earlier. He stepped over the broken bottles and hot coals of the dying bonfires.

"What a hell hole," he mumbled, moving along the wall of the motel and checking the doorways of the units, following the flickering lights he assumed were from law enforcement or an ambulance. He could see the sheriff and several EMTs stepping out of a doorway at the far end of the building.

The sheriff hurried across the littered courtyard and waved at him. "You Lawless?"

"That's right." John didn't want to waste time with small talk. "How is she?"

"She's been roughed up some, but she's doing pretty good. Mostly bruises and a cut lip. The EMTs say she's all right." He handed John the report he had filled out.

"Thank God." John hoped his knees would hold him up. As his gaze darted over the report, he swayed under the force of his anger all over again. "Kicked her, split her lip? Ripped her earrings from her ears?" He thrust the paper at the sheriff. "I want to take her home."

They talked while they walked.

Exhaling roughly, the lawman nodded. "You're just about all she would talk about so I suspect she's anxious to see you." He touched John's arm. "We'll get those bastards. Found out they are a bunch that hang around to watch for a tourist to rob. Hit and run type outfit. Your wife just happened to be in her room when they decided to break into her unit."

"They're fair game while they run like wild dogs." John looked up to see Bella following an EMT outside her room. He forgot the animals for the moment. Something wonderful was coming back into his life.

Her fragile, battered appearance hit him hard. She noticed him then and lifted her hand in silent greeting and tried to walk to him, limping with every step. He ran toward her, arms out to grab her.

He picked her up, holding her tight while she laughed and cried in a hysterical way.

"John, you came."

He held her closer, not speaking, just listening to her mumble something against his neck.

"What did you say, baby?"

"I love you, John. I love you, I love you."

It was fear talking, not Bella. "I know you do, Flower." He knew she had been scared and hurt and was feeling safe in his arms. All that didn't keep him from loving her so deeply he lost his breath with the power of that emotion.

Back in the chopper, he held her in his lap. While he buckled them in their seat, she didn't take her eyes from him and managed to hold onto him one way or another while he worked on their safety harness.

"It's okay, Bella. I won't let anything happen to you." He kissed her cheek and held her close to his heart.

He was glad as hell the pilot knew how to keep his trap shut and could fly without having a conversation. His center of focus was Bella and how bad he felt for her.

She didn't talk anymore, just stared straight ahead when she wasn't gazing at him. There were a million questions he was dying to have answers to, but he wouldn't badger her now.

The telltale blood on her nose and lips stirred his anger to cataclysmic proportions. He couldn't believe any man would want to hit Bella, much less really do it. It might take time and money, but that same man was due some pain. She looked up at him and he forced the grimace of rage from his features. He didn't want to be the cause of any more fright in her life.

Chapter Nineteen

Three weeks later, John left Bella in Ellie's capable hands and flew back to San Padre with Max to view the bodies of five goons that had drowned after stealing a boat. One of them wore Bella's crucifix and her earrings. Her handbag had been found tied to one of the thief's arms. John relished the taste of vindication. What the hell. It was revenge he tasted and it was good.

The sheriff had given John a copy of the report written up on Royal Port. The man Bella had intended to meet had missed his sail time and showed up the next night, hauling some pretty impressive pieces of art. He checked out, had a legal importing and exporting license and dealt in high dollar merchandise. He was not involved in Bella's attack. John had to see what it was that made Bella take such a risk.

"Max, while I'm down here, I'm going on to New Orleans."

"Aw, John. You're going to visit that Port son-of-a-bitch." Max waved the mortician away as he tried to hand John the earrings that had been ripped from Bella. They were not fit to touch her now. "I'll go with you."

"I'd rather go alone." John turned away from the scene of death and walked outside to the car he had rented. "I'll wait until the chopper gets to the airport to pick you up."

"I know how angry you are, John. Bella needs you out of jail more than anything else."

John grinned at his friend. "Hell, I don't plan on killing him. He lured her down here with the idea he had something she wants really bad." He raked a hand over his hair. "I aim to get it for her."

"Very noble." Max smiled wryly. "Just keep a watch on your ass while you're there."

"I intend to." He looked up when he heard the unmistakable sound of copter blades in the distance. "I hear your ride coming." He opened the car door. "Get in. I'll drive you over to the helipad."

A woman stepped out of the motel manager's office and waved at John. She walked, then ran toward them. "Mister, I have your wife's wedding ring. Found it today. The bastard's dropped it and didn't have the chance to dirty it none."

John held his hand out and the woman dropped the small circle of gold and diamonds into his palm. "You don't know what this will mean to my wife. I can't thank you enough." He reached for his wallet, but she stopped him.

"No way, mister. I just want her to get it back."

"She'll be so happy and want to thank you personally."

The woman smiled and looked down shyly. "Maybe someday." She turned and trotted back toward the office.

John slid the ring onto his pinkie finger and looked at his watch. "Time sure the hell drags when you have some place to go."

"You're anxious to get rid of me." Max smiled, apparently pleased with how the marriage was going.

"No. Anxious to get back home to Mrs. Lawless."

* * * *

Bella circled the days date with a red pen and then hid the calendar in the supply closet. She admitted to herself it was foolish to hide it. John knew perfectly well what the date was.

She looked in the bedroom door and sighed heavily. Evenings were always the worst.

Here she was, being selfish again. He had to stay on the ball when it came to his investment firm. And the trip was necessary. However, all the pep talk and reasoning in the world didn't ease her loneliness.

She wondered if he would survive her lovemaking if she let go and forced herself on him.

What would he do if she just came out and told him how much she loved him? Things had changed. She would never do that now, fearful of what she would see in his eyes.

She left the quiet bedroom and went out to the patio to sit on the glider. Roscoe lounged in the last rays of the setting sun, but immediately jumped up and ran to where she sat.

"Hello, puppy dog." She patted the space on the seat next to her. "Sit by me and we'll share a treat after dinner."

The dog hopped up on the glider to flop down beside her and gazed at her with devotion in his dark eyes. She patted his head and stroked his silky ears, drowsing and listening to the distant call of crows flying into the stand of old pine trees to roost.

Without warning, the dog jumped off the glider and she sat up, opening her eyes. It wasn't a car coming up the lane like she had hoped, only a skinny jackrabbit darting across the lawn.

Her gaze slipped to the neat little house that Buck and Ellie shared. A light shone in the living room window and Bella wondered what they were doing. Probably talking or watching a movie, eating popcorn and laughing like normal couples.

Her own soft snort of derision startled her. If she knew what normal was, she wouldn't have gone off on that wild and dangerous goose chase. Now, here she was getting ready to apologize again for her thoughtless actions.

What did she know about being responsible and all the things people scorned her for not having? She had found it so easy to turn herself over to John, to his keeping and care. She knew only one thing about herself. Her heart belonged madly, desperately, completely and eternally to him. Four years of living, of loving nothing but John. There was no other. Not ever.

Tired of staring at someone else's loving home, Bella went back inside the house. The television provided company and she needed to find the ironing board. Her search began and ended in the big pantry off the kitchen. She opened the double doors to look around the room, fragrant with spices and apples in a basket. She turned the light on and looked around with a smile. "Bonanza," she murmured.

There was an artificial tree and boxes of ornaments for it. No longer interested in ironing, she began to drag all the seasonal finery to the hearth room. To her dismay the tree proved to be too tall, its tip scraping the ceiling. Standing back to study the situation, she became too absorbed in the problem to hear the entry hall door open and close.

"Hello, beautiful."

She gasped and turned to see John smiling at her from the doorway, holding a huge bouquet of daisies and a gift-wrapped box.

"John." She sobbed his name, not caring that her voice croaked on tears and her face screwed up while she cried in her overwhelming joy. "John."

He closed the distance between them and scooped her up against his chest. "Looks like Christmas came early around here."

He had kissed her many times, but this was like the sweetest wine pouring from his lips and tongue, offering her his everything. Soft hungry desire and precious giving of himself. He held her so tight she could hardly breathe, but she didn't want it to stop. Her love was holding her again.

The scent of daisies wafted around her while he kissed her, gently, softly. She noticed the large bouquet he had in his hand. "John, daisies. How sweet…my wedding bouquet was…" Tears welled and she pressed her face to his chest.

"They're like you, sweet and beautiful." He leaned over to carefully place the box on the coffee table along with a bottle of wine he had been holding. He held her close and kissed the top of her head. "What's with the phony tree? Let's go cut a fresh one."

She laughed and stroked his hair. "It is pretty ugly."

"I'll get your coat and pick up an axe from the stable." He kissed her again, and then gazed into her eyes. "Sure you feel like going out in the fields?"

"Well, of course." There it was, the window of opportunity. "You know, John." She slipped her arms into the jacket he held out for her. "Doctor Morton said I could do anything I wanted to do now. Anything."

He was quiet for a minute and then chuckled, leaning over her shoulder to nibble her ear lobe. "I hope you're propositioning me."

Her laugh was seductive and her touch well placed on his rear. "You guessed so quickly, I'll have to give you the special prize."

"And what is that?"

"Oh, you must work for it. Come with me."

He picked up the bottle of wine and the lovely box. "Will I enjoy this work?"

"You used to."

He groaned softly. "I'll bet I haven't lost my taste for it."

"You're already making me happy." She grasped his fingers and led him out of the house and down the gravel path to the stable. "I know the perfect place to whet your taste buds."

He held onto her fingers and grinned at her. "Where are we going, my little fox?"

"To my den where we can hide in the dark and do naughty things."

"Hey, I like dark."

"And?"

"Naughty things."

She laughed and pulled him along behind her. "My nest is the sweet little stall in the very back. I furnished it myself."

"Well, hell. I can't turn down an invite like that." He quirked a brow, smiling as he pulled her back. "Got a minute to talk to me first?"

She fought a tremble of worry that wavered around her heart. "Of course. Wouldn't you like to go to my nest to do it?"

"Do it?" He grinned at her. "You're bent on seducing me."

"I'm trying." *Trying to show you how desperately I need and want you.*

"I have to explain something to you that I'm not proud of. Maybe you'd rather hear it out here."

"What I really want is you and me, back there." Dear Lord, he was trying to break it off with her in a nice way. *Please God, don't let it be so.*

"Okay, I'll make this short. I've been an all out jackass and I can't believe you're still with me." He touched his fingertip to her lips. "Four years I ran roughshod over you and all because I was hiding my inadequacies, lousy feelings of low self esteem and self doubt. I would understand perfectly if you told me to kiss your ass."

She was silent for several minutes. "You mean you aren't mad about all the evil things I did to you?" Heaven rained down one more chance for her to know and give happiness. "The long hours you waited for me in spas and dress shops? The dawn phone calls for help?" She pressed close to him and whispered, "Any other man would have left me in the desert."

"This man would never desert you." John inclined his head in the direction of the stable. "So, where exactly is that nest, foxy?"

She closed her eyes in a swell of pure bliss and sighed. "Just follow my tail and we'll break in my new straw bed." She glanced down at the things in his hand. "Gifts? You'll make a good mate."

He laughed and gently swatted her rear. "And I intend to mate with you. And mate with you, vixen."

* * * *

That wisp of worry hadn't left. The words she had wanted to say, had wanted to hear from him had not been spoken. Bella still worried about where she fit in John's life even as they ran inside the stable, laughing in their delicious taste of rising passion.

She led him down the gravel path to the stable and they went inside. The interior was dimly lit and smelled of horses, fresh sweet mash, clean straw and alfalfa. The horses seemed content to munch their food and mostly ignored their presence. Nothing else mattered, not even the missing words now that he picked her up and carried her to the stall she pointed out.

"John." Her trembling arms clasped him as tightly as she could manage while her lips played over his. "John, I love saying your name."

"We're home, baby." He brushed his lips over hers and let her down to stand on her feet. "I'm anxious to see what's under that sexy little fox thing you're wearing." Like royalty, he sank down in the thick straw and leaned back to watch her disrobe.

A rose flush warmed her body. He had said the right thing to put her in her element. Show and tell, tease and tantalize.

She stood over him, facing the wall, and moved her hips from side to side, wanting to fall on him while his hand moved up her calf to the sensitive place on her inner thigh. Resisting a complete implosion of will, she dropped her jacket over him. He smiled, arching his brows in approval.

It took all her willpower to slowly work the knit sheath dress off her body and let it drop onto his face. The lace panties, he caught in his fist as they drifted down on the warm air. Looking over her shoulder at him, she snapped her fingers. "Now you."

He reached up and pulled her down beside him, then got to his feet. Watching him, she could hardly breathe. He was simply beautiful. She could only feel.

"You don't have to beg me to get naked." He unbuttoned his shirt too slowly for Bella. She forced herself to keep quiet and enjoyed his tease. The more skin he revealed the more intense her sexual need became.

The shirt was gone and his slacks were in the corner with his shorts, tie and shoes. Bella groaned aloud with impatience while he stripped his socks off and his erection jutted up to press proud and wide against his belly.

"John, come here." She couldn't hold it back another second. Right or wrong time or if it never came, she had to tell him. "Before we make love."

He sank down on the straw with her, drawing her leg over his waist. "Sounds serious."

"I am seriously in love with you, John." She curled into his strong body and kissed his chest. "I love you so much nothing else matters. I can't see or feel anything but you. Only you."

He looked into her eyes and answered in a steady deep voice. "I love you, Bella Fleur Lawless." She wept when he took her wedding ring from his finger and slipped it back onto hers. "With all my heart, I love you. I don't want a divorce and I don't believe you do." He spread his shirt over her and then pulled the fancy wrapped box to where they lay. "Merry early Christmas."

Her fingers worked feverishly on the ribbons and fancy paper and shook visibly while she reached into the nest of tissue paper. Her mouth opened in stunned disbelief and she mutely gazed at the treasure in her hand. The yard light beamed in through the window and caught in the heavy blue and gold crystal chalices and twinkled gloriously over her face.

She burst into tears and crumpled against him. He held her without interfering in her emotional privacy, kissing her and whispering words of love. Long moments and many waves of tears came and went while she poured out her heart to him, revealed all her sorrow and grief and her love for him. He wiped his eyes and held her tight, willing his love to replace her pain.

Finally, she could talk to him without sobbing.

"I am the most blessed woman in the world." She rose up to her knees and hugged his neck. "Thank you, my husband. I do love you so very much."

"That's what I want, Bella. To make you happy for as long as I live." He opened the bottle of wine, and offered it to her. "I forgot glasses."

"I think my parents would want us to toast our love in the proper way."

She handed him both chalices and he poured wine into them. After sipping from her wine, she held it to his lips, smiling as he drank. He repeated the action, letting her sip from his wine.

Her voice was soft as a sigh. "We are forever bound."

He kissed her, letting her taste the wine on his lips. "Forever, my Flower. Forever."

THE END

Siren Publishing, Inc.
www.SirenPublishing.com

LaVergne, TN USA
12 January 2010
169800LV00004B/26/P

9 781606 015094